# THE NEW LORD WESTLAKE

Camilla Brentwood's dear friend is the Honourable Timothy Harding. When Tim's grandfather, Lord Westlake, dies, he's shocked to discover he might lose his inheritance. It seems that Lord Westlake had another son who was sent away in disgrace, following a series of scandalous incidents . . . Camilla, out riding, is displeased when Jack Somergill 'saves' her from injury. She wonders who this stranger can be, little knowing that if Jack's plans succeed, he will surprise all of Kelsham — including Camilla . . .

KAREN ABBOTT

# THE NEW LORD WESTLAKE

*Complete and Unabridged*

## LINFORD
*Leicester*

First published in Great Britain in 2010

First Linford Edition
published 2011

British Library CIP Data

Abbott, Karen.
   The new Lord Westlake. - -
(Linford romance library)
1. Aristocracy (Social class)- -Fiction.
2. Inheritance and succession- -Fiction.
3. Love stories. 4. Large type books.
I. Title II. Series
823.9′2–dc22

ISBN 978–1–44480–526–0

Published by
F. A. Thorpe (Publishing)
Anstey, Leicestershire

Set by Words & Graphics Ltd.
Anstey, Leicestershire
Printed and bound in Great Britain by
T. J. International Ltd., Padstow, Cornwall

This book is printed on acid-free paper

# 1

The moment the carriage drew to a halt, Camilla Brentwood jumped down onto the flagged forecourt of Kelsham Hall, the country seat of the late departed Lord Westlake, and hurried up the stone steps to the pillared frontage, where she beat a staccato rhythm on the door with the brass knocker. As the door opened, the sombre face of the late Lord Westlake's butler reflected the reality of his lordship's recent demise.

'A distressing time, Miss Brentwood,' he agreed sorrowfully, standing back to allow her entry, knowing that this visitor had no need of social protocol. She had run wild at Kelsham Hall for the past twelve years or more — ever since her riding skills had enabled her to out-distance her governess in order to follow her older brother Ralph on his frequent jaunts onto Westlake land in order to pursue his friendship with Lord Westlake's grandson, Timothy Harding.

'You will find Mr Timothy in the library,' the butler directed her kindly.

Camilla hurried down the hallway, leaving Russell to attend to the more formal duty of welcoming and announcing her mama. Since those happy carefree days of childhood, two years at Miss Marshall's Seminary For The Daughters of Gentlemen in nearby Bristol had smoothed away many external rough edges of her character — but her inner being was unaffected by most of the airs and graces she had learned to adopt, much to her dear mama's despair. Not even pausing to knock, she entered the library and ran towards the sombre figure of the Honourable Timothy Harding.

Dressed in black, he was looking up at the likeness of Godfrey Harding, his late grandfather — a portrait that showed the elderly man to be both proud and handsome, with a hint of roguishness in his piercing blue eyes.

'Tim! I'm so sorry. We came as soon

as we could.' Her hands reached out to him in heartfelt compassion. 'You must be feeling absolutely bereft!'

The sadness in Tim's eyes lifted fractionally as he turned to greet her and drew her into a brotherly embrace. After a brief hug, they parted.

'I knew you would come — though I did not expect you to cut short your season. How many broken hearts have you left behind?'

'Twenty at least, if their declarations are to be believed!' countered Camilla lightly. 'But, since none of them caused my heart to even miss a beat, I left with no regrets.'

They grinned at each other, remembering her declared determination before her departure to London not to become betrothed unless her heart was captured completely.

'But did you have a good time?'

'It was wonderful,' Camilla confessed. 'So many balls, routs and parties! And lots of beaux falling over themselves to make an impression. But it became wearisome after a while, and I felt so confined in the city. We were shepherded around like sheep, and hardly ever had chance to ride.'

Tim smiled his sympathy, then, with some unspoken instinct, both turned back to the portrait, Tim's gaze resting on the blue eyes twinkling out at him.

'I miss him so much,' he said simply.

Camilla squeezed the hand she still held. 'But he was ready to go, Tim,' she comforted him. 'He had a good life. Were you with him at the end?'

Tim nodded, his expression sad. 'Yes. It was just after dinner. He thought it was indigestion and would not let me send for Dr Morris. I wish I had . . . But I doubt it would have made any difference. It seemed as though he wanted to tell me something, but another pain swept over him. He just said, 'I'm sorry, Tim,' and he was gone.' He looked at Camilla and something in his eyes caused a wave of concern to sweep over her.

'What is it, Tim? What's the matter?'

Tim gave a harsh laugh. 'I think I now know what he wanted to tell me.'

He took hold of both her hands and looked steadily into her eyes. 'The fact is, Camilla, it seems that I may not be the new Lord Westlake. Apparently, Grandfather had another son — born before my father. Nobody has heard from him for thirty years or more but, if he is still alive, he is my grandfather's heir . . . and his descendants after him.'

Once Camilla's mother, Eleanor, had joined them, it did not take long for Tim to tell them all he knew.

'It seems Grandfather's elder son is called Tarquin,' he explained. 'He was a wild young man and there were scandals upon scandals, until one day he went too far.

'He was twenty-five years of age and was spending much of his time in London, gambling away Grandfather's money in wild and reckless living. One night, he and his cronies had been drinking heavily and they abducted a young woman whom they . . . ' He paused, then, glancing apologetically at both ladies, said carefully, ' . . . treated badly. The girl's father discovered the outrage and tried to rescue his daughter. There was an exchange of gunfire, and both the girl and her father were killed.

'Tarquin and his friends were never seen again. Grandfather apparently made what amends he could to the unfortunate widow and declared his son dead. He never spoke his name again, nor allowed anyone else to do so.'

'I think we all assumed Tarquin had died as he had lived,' Eleanor mused. 'It was thought that he had taken part in many a duel, though none dared to say so openly, of course, and we respected Godfrey's wishes far too much to ask him for details when he announced Tarquin's death.'

Tim nodded his understanding before continuing. 'It is now known that Grandfather despatched him to America with instructions never to return. From then on, Grandfather treated my father as his heir — until, of course, he and my mother were killed in that dreadful carriage accident.'

'Yes, the whole local population was

devastated,' Eleanor remembered, wringing her gloved hands. 'We mourned them as the loss of Lord Westlake's heir and his wife! And you were such a young child.'

Camilla had listened, spellbound. 'So, is this Tarquin still alive?'

Tim shrugged. 'No one seems to know. Grandfather's solicitors are to send men to America to see if they can trace him.'

'But if he is alive and comes back, surely he will be arrested?' Camilla persisted, not wanting to imagine Timothy being denied his right to inherit his grandfather's title and all that went with it. 'Wouldn't he be charged with murder and hanged? So you would inherit anyway.'

'Maybe, but he might have an heir — and that heir would take precedence over me.' Tim smiled, somewhat ruefully. 'It seems that Grandfather never actually disinherited Tarquin officially. I suppose he could not bring himself to do it.' He twisted his mouth wryly. 'No doubt, it will give our esteemed neighbours something to gossip about over the next few weeks.'

That prediction proved to be correct. Many of the older generation remembered the scandal that had lain dormant for the remainder of Godfrey Harding's life. Speculation was rife, and the grand funeral that took place a few days later was attended by scores of town dignitaries and their wives.

After the majority of the guests had departed, Tim told Camilla that he was removing himself to London for two weeks or so, in order to avoid some of the more insensitive and garrulous bearers of condolences — and also to be closer to his grandfather's lawyers, Cribb and Langford of Westminster.

★   ★   ★

It was just over two weeks later that Tim returned and drove over to Greenacres. He found Camilla and her mother at home and was ushered into their drawing room, where he was warmly welcomed.

'How are you, Tim?' Eleanor asked, thinking regretfully how pleasant it would have been to have him as her son-in-law. It was all very well, Camilla laughing indignantly at such a suggestion, protesting that they were far too good friends to contemplate marrying each other! 'Has anything been resolved?' she added.

'I am afraid not, ma'am. I have had so many meetings with Grandfather's man of business and his lawyers that my head is spinning,' Tim confessed. 'It seems that, after my parents died, Grandfather sent men to try to discover Tarquin's whereabouts. They traced him to a town not far from New York, where they discovered he had joined the army. However, no further information was available and it was presumed he had deserted the army and was perhaps living under an assumed name. Grandfather's lawyers have now sent investigators back to America to try to pick up the trail.'

'What will you do if your uncle is traced and is able to take up his inheritance?' Camilla asked. 'Surely he would let you stay at Kelsham Hall. It has always been your family home.'

Tim shook his head. 'Grandfather has left me a property in Leicestershire, so I shall not be homeless, but I do not plan to take it over immediately. In fact, that is really what I have come to tell you. It might be years before the matter is settled. I cannot stand this waiting about, one minute hoping to hear my disgraced uncle has met his nemesis and the next expecting that he has not. So I have made up my mind to get on with my life.'

He paused. 'I have decided to join the army, like your brother Ralph. I have applied to join his regiment. He finds it very fulfilling, does he not?'

Camilla, devastated by this announcement, struggled to keep her composure as she answered his question. 'I expect so, though we have not seen him for over a year. He makes it seem quite exciting in his letters, though I am sure life on the Spanish Peninsula must be particularly hard — and hundreds of men are killed in every battle. It must be quite terrifying!' She sighed, inwardly acknowledging how much she missed her elder brother. 'I think it helps him forget about his disappointment over Emily, my former school friend. He was devastated, you remember, when she broke off their engagement and refused to see him again.'

Tim smiled brightly. 'Then he will, no doubt, encourage me to get over this disappointment in the same way that he has got over his. Pickford, Grandfather's man of business, says that there is enough money in my settlement to purchase a commission. If everything goes according to plan, I shall be there by Christmas.'

Now Camilla could not hide her distress. 'Oh, Tim! You are my dearest friend. I shall miss you — and all our rides together.' She pouted prettily, trying to make light of it. 'I shall have to become ladylike and merely take gentle exercise in the park once you are gone.'

Tim took both her hands. 'No, you will not. You must still ride on our land and, when you see me next, I shall have such tales to tell you!'

# 2

Camilla laughed in sheer joy as her mare thundered over the tufted meadow, the breeze stinging her rosy cheeks. Nearly two years had passed since Lord Westlake's demise, followed by Tim's departure. Camilla had enjoyed another London season, but without losing her heart to any of the beaux or dandies. She was thankful that neither of her parents had insisted that she repay their outlay of money by agreeing to an advantageous but loveless marriage.

Their quiet life on the outskirts of Bath had been turned upside down by the arrival home of her brother, Ralph, who had suffered serious injuries at the Battle of Badajoz at the beginning of April. He was now making an excellent recovery and hoped to be fit enough soon to rejoin his unit in Portugal. Tim, he reported, was doing well and was already advancing his career, having recently been promoted to lieutenant.

The month of June was nearly over, and the sun was shining. Camilla had spent time sitting with Ralph, who was resting on a seat in the shaded part of their garden.

'Go for a ride, Camilla,' he had urged her. 'I know you must be longing to do so, and I do not see why you should be denied the pleasure just because Dr Morris has not yet given me leave to ride again.'

Riding her mare had been Camilla's main release from the hours of enforced inactivity. That, and visiting her friends, which Ralph had also insisted she must do; visits to the town's Pump Room and Tea Rooms, where she walked arm-in-arm with Susannah Morris, the doctor's daughter, or Lottie Marshall, the parson's daughter, their heads bent close together as they discussed fashions and young men and how long it would be before the new Lord Westlake appeared to take up his inheritance. Though Camilla still cherished the hope that Tim might yet be declared the new lord.

Oh, but it was her wild gallops that cleared away the cobwebs of weeks of subdued moods when Ralph was very ill . . . and then more weeks of hovering around the downstairs room adapted for his convalescence, now that he was recovering. Not for one minute had she resented her time being taken by such matters — but she did enjoy her daily rides.

On this sunny afternoon she had ridden her mare hard for almost an hour, trailed by Jeffries, their stable lad, and it was time to be heading home. She laughed out loud in exhilaration as she set Mayfly in line for the hawthorn hedge that separated their smaller acreage from the expanse of Westlake land — for here she was, riding astride in a pair of Ralph's long-discarded breeches, her hair tucked into a masculine riding hat . . . and was about to soar into the air!

Her heart beat faster in anticipation as she leaned forward over Mayfly's arched neck, rising in the stirrups in preparation for the jump. As her pace increased, she became vaguely aware of hooves pounding the turf in her wake and she felt a moment's surprise that the stable lad, Jeffries, was keeping pace with her. He was usually content merely to keep her in his sight, knowing that his charge was the best horsewoman in the district.

With a slight dig of her heels, she urged her mare on. The only sounds were the drumming hooves of the two horses — and, maybe, the pounding of her heart as she abandoned herself to the absolute delight of thundering towards the hedge. Then, in the next instant, she felt as though her breath had been sucked out of her body as a strong arm clamped around her waist, totally unseating her as she was drawn back against a firm masculine body. A deep voice murmured, 'All is well! You are safe now. Relax against me!'

Relax? Was the man out of his mind? He had dragged her off her horse and he expected her to relax?

'Let me go this instant!' she snarled at him, struggling to twist her body round to face her captor. She was seated on the hard front edge of his saddle and it was most uncomfortable.

The man's hold of her relaxed slightly, though he still held her securely. A part of her mind marvelled at his control of his mount, since both his hands were employed in holding her, but she dismissed the burgeoning admiration and concentrated on her indignation as she managed to face him. His attire was not quite that of a gentleman, and his strange accent puzzled her.

'What do you think you are doing?' she cried. 'Put me down at once!'

The pace was slowing as her furious gaze locked with brilliant blue eyes that seemed out of place in the sun-bronzed face. The glimmer of concern in those eyes slowly changed to a gleam of wry humour, and she thought for a moment that he might take her at her word and drop her there and then. But he did not, and she continued to glare at him.

'Is that a fit way to address your rescuer, ma'am?' he asked lightly. 'You would never have cleared that hedge. You could have been killed.'

'I jump that hedge nearly every day!' Camilla shot back. 'As you would have seen, had you minded your own business and not mine. Besides, you are trespassing on private land. Rein in and lower me to the ground.'

Obligingly the man drew to a smooth halt and, gripping the heaving sides of his mount with his knees, he leaned to the side and lowered Camilla gently to the ground. Her legs were trembling and she almost stumbled. But the man had dismounted in a swift fluid motion, without, it seemed, having quite let go of her, and he now towered over her, holding her steady.

As their bodies touched, she could feel his heart beating against her and she was almost tempted, just for a moment — purely in order to recover her composure, she assured herself — to lean against his taut frame. But some inner instinct warned her that a moment's support accepted from his very masculine body would be a moment too long. She took a step backwards, as if seared by an intense heat.

She realised that the man was eyeing her mode of attire, and that he seemed puzzled by its incongruity. Aware that the breeches hugged her slim hips and left nothing of her shape to the imagination, she felt a faint wave of heat flow over her cheeks. In defiant reaction to it, she took another step away from him and stood in a challenging pose with the backs of her hands on her hips.

'Have you never seen a woman in breeches before?' she felt constrained to snap, even though it would have been wiser not to.

The man cupped his chin between his thumb and forefinger and continued to appraise her figure, his lips beginning to curl upwards.

'Well, ma'am, now that you ask that, I must admit that I have . . . but none quite so shapely as you.'

Camilla's cheeks burned more fiercely. 'How dare you! I demand an apology for your insolence!'

The man grinned unashamedly. 'Oh, no apology, ma'am, except to your ruffled feelings, for I truly believed you to be in danger of your own folly. And as to my remark about your figure, I simply answered your question.'

'A gentleman would not have responded so!' Camilla retorted.

'And a lady would not have asked,' the man replied, quirking an eyebrow. 'However, I have always tried to live as a gentleman and I am mighty pleased to make your acquaintance.'

'You have not made my acquaintance!' Camilla snapped, her eyes flashing dangerously.

'Then I must rectify that immediately.' He swept his hat off his head with a bow that would have graced any courtly gathering. 'Jack Somergill . . . at your service, ma'am.'

Camilla was not at all sure that she

wished to disclose her name to this forward young man. Her mama would have a blue fit if she knew how she was dressed, and she thought it more circumspect to remain incognito. She was relieved to realise that Jeffries was cantering towards them with Mayfly on a short rein.

'Ah, here is my groom. So I will bid you good day, sir,' she said stiffly. She turned to her horse and took hold of the reins, uneasy at the stranger witnessing her masculine mode of mounting — but, wearing her brother's breeches and using his saddle, she had no alternative. She paused, partly to postpone the moment of mounting and partly because she was aware of her own ungraciousness in the face of what she hoped had been a genuine mistake on his part. And, although she doubted his claim to be a gentleman, she ought not forget that she had been reared to behave as a lady.

'I suppose I must thank you for your intervention, however mistaken,' she

20

said grudgingly. To make some amends for her lack of manners, she added, 'Are you staying in the area?'

He laughed, obviously aware of her ploy to alleviate her conscience. 'Oh, yes, I am staying nearby,' he answered, somewhat enigmatically. He swiftly remounted his horse with an ease that filled her with reluctant admiration, and tipped his hat forward a little in a farewell salute. 'Until we meet again.'

Camilla watched until he had ridden out of sight, uncomfortably aware that, as well as being 'caught' in incommodious dress, she hadn't behaved as well as she might have done. As to their meeting again — she felt that was extremely unlikely.

★ ★ ★

Jack Somergill rode away grinning hugely. Although inexperienced in the ways of the nobility and so-called high 'ton' of society, he realised that the young lady was of a higher level than he

21

had at first supposed from her clothing. In fact, from a distance, he had thought it was a youth he was about to rescue — until he had felt the roundness of her breasts when he had seized hold of her from behind. To which of the respectable neighbouring families did she belong? No doubt he would find out before too long, if his assessment of this small spa town were correct.

He recalled what the land agent had said to him — that, although it had only a modest spring compared to neighbouring Bath, Kelsham's well of invigorating waters was sufficiently known that it attracted a goodly number of visitors. Thus, the town was able to boast an Assembly Room; a posting inn; a lending library; a number of highly esteemed shops; an attractive open park; and enough families of independent means to form a convivial society and give employment to those less fortunate than themselves. All of which ensured that Kelsham was not the backwater it might otherwise have been.

Used as he was to the wide open spaces of America's vast plains, Jack was optimistic that he might indeed make his main dwelling here, where, in addition to the farms rented out to local tenants, he now owned many acres of parkland and untamed countryside. There were also many miles of fishing rights along the banks of the River Avon as it flowed on its way to Bristol and the open sea. One thing was sure; he was looking forward to a quieter and more peaceful existence than he had experienced in London during the closing weeks of its society season.

Not that he had pushed himself to the forefront of society. Wanting to maintain his privacy until he had taken up his inheritance and established himself among his new neighbours, he had preferred to remain in the background, and had dressed as plainly as any sober businessman of comfortable means might do.

A few rather alarming mothers and chaperones had shown an initial interest in him but, since he was using the name he had grown up believing to be his, it did not take them long to decide that his lack of flair must inevitably reflect a lack of money — and had consequently looked for other fish to hook. It would not be the same here.

He had enjoyed the final days of his present anonymity, but knew he could not delay announcing his presence for much longer. The worthy gentlemen of Cribb and Langford knew he was here, as did Pickford, his land agent, and Russell, his late grandfather's butler. And, although he had used only the name Jack Somergill during his inconspicuous visits to town over the previous few days, his appointment with Mr Josiah Hurley, the manager of the town's only bank, was set for ten o'clock the following morning. Following that, he knew, his quiet life would be over.

He smiled grimly as he recalled his preliminary visit to the local bank earlier that day, when his request to see the manager had been met with a haughty refusal.

The clerk had looked down his rather pointed nose at Jack's nondescript attire before informing him in superior tones, 'Mr Hurley is far too busy to allow unscheduled interruptions to intrude upon his work. If you will give me your personal details and tell me how much money you wish to deposit with us, I will make an appointment for you — shall we say a week from today?'

Jack had replied pleasantly, 'You have my name. I shall return tomorrow morning at five minutes past ten o'clock and will expect to be shown into Mr Hurley's office at that time. Good day to you!' The scowling clerk was left to gape at his retreating back.

Tomorrow there would be no more of the drab, nondescript outerwear of the previous few days. He would be dressed in the impeccable attire he had purchased in London and would be driving his newly-bought fashionable curricle drawn by matching bays, as befitted the new Lord Westlake.

He grinned again, wondering what

the little firebrand he had just met
would make of him when next their
paths crossed!

# 3

The following day, Eleanor Brentwood was presiding over a small gathering in her drawing room at Greenacres, her family home, when the butler brought in a letter on a silver tray that he lowered at her side.

'Thank you, Norris. Is a reply needed?'

'Not immediately, madam.' He laid the tray on a spindle-legged table at Eleanor's side and discreetly left the room. Eleanor returned her attention to her guests. Various topics had been aired, and no characters irrevocably assassinated. Any thoughts that might have been censorious were kept from utterance by the presence of Jane Yardley, the vicar's wife, whose only fault was that she assumed her friends to be as sweet-natured as herself.

The ladies' melodious conversation

was overshadowed by the more lively voices from the other end of the drawing room, where her guests' sons and daughters of drawing room age were holding court around a cushioned couch where Ralph was resting. Merry peals of laughter punctuated the air.

'Do open the note, Eleanor,' urged Bessie Houghton, wife of the local magistrate, regarding the folded missive through her lorgnette. 'I am sure that is Violet's handwriting. It may give the reason for her absence. It is not like her to miss one of your afternoons. Something must have occurred to prevent her coming.' Her eyes glimmered with anticipation at the thought that a tasty morsel of gossip could in the offing.

'Maybe she is feeling unwell?' Martha Morris, the doctor's wife, suggested. 'Perhaps one of us might call on the way home?'

'Well!' Eleanor exclaimed in some annoyance, lowering the note to her lap and looking at her guests. 'Violet will be full of herself after this!'

The attention of the other three women was captivated immediately.

'What is it, Eleanor? What has Violet done to upset you?' Jane Yardley enquired gently.

'I am not upset!' Eleanor declared, somewhat untruthfully. 'Yes, I suppose I am,' she amended, with an apologetic glance at the vicar's wife. 'She has stolen a march on us, that's what she has done!'

Bessie leaned forward eagerly and placed her cup upon the table in front of her. 'Stolen a march on us? In what way? Oh, do tell us what she says!'

Eleanor glanced around at the eagerly expectant faces. 'Well, according to Violet, it seems the new Lord Westlake has come to take up his inheritance at last! And Violet has got knowledge of his arrival and seized the opportunity to arrange a dinner party in his honour.'

'Lord Westlake? He's *here*? In Kelsham?'

'When did he arrive?'

'Has anyone else seen him?'

All else was forgotten. Teacups were

abandoned, and the ladies gazed at each other in a mixture of excitement and a little of Eleanor's indignation that such an event had occurred without any of them knowing about it.

Eleanor perused the note in her hand. 'She says she learned of his arrival only this morning, after he had . . . and I quote . . . 'graced dear Josiah's bank with his illustrious presence'.' Really! How Violet loves to use effusive words. And so, she goes on to say, she invites our family to dinner tomorrow evening at Larkspur Lodge to make his acquaintance and to welcome him to our 'humble yet prestigious town'.' Eleanor ran her eyes down the remainder of the note. ''Just a select gathering,' she says. 'Nothing formal'.'

'Hmm — arranged with almost indecent haste!' Bessie Houghton commented, adding astutely, 'That is so that none of us could visit, nor arrange anything to pre-empt her. Huh — all we can do now is leave our cards! I shall tell Mr Houghton to call without delay.'

'We might be invited, too,' Jane Yardley suggested mildly.

'I doubt it,' Bessie rejoined. 'Violet hopes to steal a march on us all. She will be pushing her daughter to the fore and won't want too many rivals for his lordship's attention. Dorothea is not exactly a diamond of the first water, is she? And she has seen more seasons than she cares to remember!'

'And we all know, Eleanor, that she has her eye on your Camilla for her George, now that Timothy Harding is no longer a contender,' Martha Morris pointed out sagely. 'No, it will be a very select number, mark my words.'

'I wonder if any of the young people have heard whisper of Lord Westlake's arrival,' Eleanor murmured. 'Though I am sure they would have informed us, if that were so.' She beckoned, and caught Camilla's attention. 'Camilla, dear, can you spare us a moment?'

Camilla had just been about to relate her meeting with the trespassing Jack

Somergill, knowing that any new face, especially a handsome young one, would be an excellent diversion. Instead, she excused herself from the younger group and crossed the room towards her mother.

'Have any of the young people heard anything of the arrival of the new Lord Westlake?' Eleanor asked as she drew near. 'It seems he is already in residence, and none of us knew about it!'

'No, Mama,' Camilla answered at once. 'No one has said anything — and I am sure they would have done, had a new face been seen in the district. Oh!' Her cheeks took on a rosy hue. An image of the handsome Jack Somergill swam into her mind. Surely not? No, if he were Lord Westlake, his name would be Jack Harding, would it not? And his attire had not been that of a wealthy lord of the realm. In addition, he was too young. Even so, her expression betrayed the fact that something out of the ordinary had occurred — some incident she had not thought fit to share with her mama.

'Camilla?' her mama queried, knowing her daughter well enough to know that something significant had caused Camilla's sudden confusion.

Camilla glanced back to the group of young people who were now looking curiously their way. The girls — Susannah Morris, Charlotte and Kate Yardley, and Leticia Houghton — detached themselves from the young men and drifted towards Camilla.

'I was . . . er . . . just about to tell the others that I had seen someone new whilst I was out riding yesterday,' she said hesitantly, not daring to look her mama in the eye, since, unfortunately, her mama had seen how she was dressed on her return from riding. 'But there was nothing to suggest that he was the new Lord Westlake. In fact, I thought he was trespassing on Lord Westlake's land.'

'And, no doubt, you told him so!' Eleanor sighed in exasperation.

'Well, yes . . . but he did not say he had the right to be there. Nor did he suggest that maybe it was I who was trespassing, since he would not know that Tim had said I might ride there!'

Eleanor rolled her eyes heavenward.

'But what did he look like?' Bessie Houghton asked eagerly. 'Did he have a look of Godfrey Harding?'

'I noticed no resemblance,' Camilla admitted. 'But now I think of it . . . ' She paused as her mind began to accept the embarrassing possibility. Her eyes widened and her cheeks glowed. 'He did have extremely blue eyes, like the portrait of Lord Westlake in his library.' *Startlingly blue* eyes, she amended inwardly.

'Then, could he be the old Lord Westlake's son Tarquin, do you think?' Mrs Houghton suggested, her eyes agog with excitement. 'What a stir his return will cause!'

'Is he handsome?' Charlotte Yardley interjected, earning herself a frown of reproof from her mama.

Her younger sister Kate pouted her lips. 'But he'll be old! Far too old to be considered handsome!' she scorned.

The older ladies raised their eyebrows in amusement at the prejudice of youth. *Too old to be handsome,* indeed!

'What did you make of him, Camilla? Did he look the gentleman?' Mrs Morris asked.

'He was . . . courteous enough,' Camilla reluctantly agreed, squirming as she remembered she had challenged his right to call himself a gentleman.

'So, he could be the new Lord Westlake?' Bessie Houghton persisted. 'Was he about the right age? Er, similar to your papa, perhaps?'

Camilla knew she was about to cause a stir. She glanced around and spread her hands in an apologetic gesture.

'That is the reason why I did not suspect he might be Lord Westlake,' she continued, all eyes back upon her, 'because he was not old at all. No more than in his late twenties, or thirty at the most! So, maybe the man I saw is not Lord Westlake at all. Maybe he is his agent, or his man of business?'

'Or his son?' suggested Mrs Houghton.

That idea started another buzz of conjecture altogether. In fact, it was quite the liveliest of afternoon tea parties that the present company had known for many a long year, and their reluctance to break up the discussion and depart was only offset by the eagerness of the visitors to repair to their homes to discover if they, too, had been honoured by an invitation to meet the new lord and discover his exact identity.

# 4

The news of the arrival of the new Lord Westlake spread swiftly throughout Kelsham and by the following morning, it was unlikely that there was a single household of note in the entire district that did not know of it. By breakfast time, it was known that the new Lord Westlake was the grandson of the old lord, and that he had come with only his valet, thus dashing any hope that Camilla might be entertaining that her 'stranger' was a mere underling.

To the ladies, it was the event of the season. For the new lord of Kelsham Hall was handsome, young and single . . . and would it not be his duty to beget an heir? And, in order to do that, he must seek and choose a wife!

The gentlemen received the news in a more prosaic manner, wondering if the new incumbent would be a huntsman and open up his land, as the previous lord had been wont to do; and would he perhaps reintroduce grouse or pheasants to his land or copses, all of which had fallen by the wayside in the latter years of his well-liked predecessor.

Arthur Brentwood's main comment regarding the arrival was, 'About time, too! Pickford has been too lax of late. I know for a fact that Dutton's farm is running at a loss, through no fault of his own, and a number of Westlake's tenants will have problems this coming winter if the necessary repairs aren't made to their property. I hope he's the sort of fellow who will listen to wise advice, and act upon it without too much delay.'

Camilla had arranged with Susannah, Charlotte, Kate and Leticia to meet at the Assembly Rooms that afternoon where tea and a selection of scones, cakes and pastries were served three times a week. Since the visiting mamas had repaired to their own homes as swiftly as was polite the previous afternoon, in order to discover if they were amongst the ones Violet Hurley considered worthy of being included in a 'select gathering', there had been no time for any of the younger ladies to press Camilla for more details. Naturally, they wanted to know as much as possible.

'Though I don't see why they are getting so excited!' Camilla had exclaimed indignantly to Ralph, after their mama's tea party had broken up. 'I have no intention of joining the throng who will be setting their caps at him. Nor of even liking him, since it is he who has displaced Tim from his inheritance and caused him to run away and join the army where he is now risking his life for our country.'

'Tim wouldn't thank you for saying so,' Ralph returned. 'Army life makes men out of boys, and though some may regret their choice, Tim assures me he doesn't.' He fixed his sister with a candid eye. 'And I am counting the days until my return to my regiment.

Society life holds little joy for me.'

Camilla regarded him compassionately. 'Are you truly over your disappointment with Emily? I know how hurt you were at the time.'

'Let's say I have learned that there is more to life than falling in love,' Ralph prevaricated in a tone that told Camilla he would not be drawn further on that personal matter. 'But, to get back to Lord Westlake: his father was the elder son, therefore he is the rightful heir. Tim accepts it with no hard feelings, and so, I suggest, should you.'

Camilla knew that what Ralph was saying made sense, but her stubborn loyalty to Tim was too dear to her heart for her to let go of it readily. Jack Somergill, if he were indeed the new Lord Westlake — and, if he were, why was his name not Harding? — was an arrogant upstart and she would let him know that that was how she regarded him!

Nevertheless, she dressed in a pretty, pale pink, elegantly trimmed carriage dress and twirled a matching parasol over her shoulder as she was driven into Kelsham that afternoon — and kept a sharp lookout for a glimpse of Jack Somergill. If they chanced to meet, she could show him that she did know how to dress properly — and she would then take a personal satisfaction in 'cutting' him!

Her friends reported gloomily that invitations to the dinner party had not been extended to their families and, after Camilla had given her friends an edited account of her encounter with the man she now supposed to be the new lord, they had to agree that their curiosity about him would not be satisfied until a future date. Charlotte, Kate and Leticia departed in the Houghtons' carriage, driven by Leticia's brother, Lionel; and Susannah, who had dismissed her family's carriage on her arrival in case it was needed by her father in the course of his duties as the local doctor, was welcomed into the Brentwood carriage for the drive home.

Susannah glanced wistfully over her shoulder as the Houghton carriage drew away.

'You'll see him again tomorrow!' Camilla teased, knowing that her friend had a fondness for Lionel, and he for her.

Susannah settled back with a contented sigh. 'He is divinely handsome, is he not?' she said dreamily.

'Exceedingly,' Camilla replied dryly.

Susannah giggled and lowered her lashes, her cheeks a rosy pink. 'He makes my heart race just to see him. Just wait, someone will do the same to you one day!' She glanced sideways at Camilla. 'George Hurley likes you,' she teased. 'Doesn't he make your heart flutter?'

'Only with annoyance,' Camilla returned. 'He takes obnoxious liberties. One of these days I shall . . . Oh!' She had just caught sight of a fine curricle drawn by a pair of matching bays approaching along the road. Her eyes were instinctively drawn to the handsome young man who was handling the reins with a casual skill. She felt a surprising jerk somewhere deep inside her as she recognised him. In the same instant, he glanced her way and lifted his hand to tip his hat in her direction, a wide grin on his face.

Camilla stiffened immediately. 'Do not look at him!' she hissed at Susannah, agitatedly twirling her parasol around as she tilted her nose skyward and settled her gaze somewhere in the region of her coachman's left ear.

'Do not look at who?' Susannah asked, craning her neck to catch sight of whoever had caused Camilla to act so strangely. Her eyes widened. 'Oh! Is that *him*? Is that Lord Westlake?'

The carriages drew level and then passed by. Susannah twisted around, her eyes fixed now on the back of Lord Westlake's head. 'I see what you mean. He *is* handsome, isn't he?'

'I told you not to look!' Camilla reproved her testily. 'He has a high enough opinion of himself as it is!'

'Oh, ho?' Susannah smiled knowingly. 'Are you sure no one has yet made your heart flutter?'

'Do not be ridiculous!' Camilla snapped. 'I hardly know the man! Nor do I intend to!'

'No, of course not.' Susannah smiled. 'But you will tell me everything about tonight, won't you?'

'Hmph!' was the only reply from her friend.

Jack Somergill drove on his way, smiling broadly. So, the little firebrand did know how to dress like a lady! More than likely, she was indeed the daughter of his neighbours, the Brentwoods, as Russell had suggested from his description. And, no doubt, he would make her acquaintance at the Hurleys' dinner party that evening. Her friend was pretty, too. A true English rose. Yes, he was looking forward to the evening's dinner party.

\* \* \*

Camilla wondered whether to plead a headache and evade officially meeting

Lord Westlake under the eagle eyes of the banker's wife, but she suspected her mama might see through her ruse, and she did not wish to make her think that her first meeting with the man had been worse than it really was. She decided to wear her favourite cornflower-blue silk gown. It was quite plain, apart from its scalloped neckline edged with eyelets that were threaded through with a dark blue velvet ribbon. It had small puff sleeves, and a wider bow of the same coloured ribbon hung down her back from the high waist. Her only other adornment was a matching velvet ribbon around her slender neck with a front-fastening clasp of deep sapphires. Not that she wanted to impress anyone, of course. It was just that, in a potentially stressful situation, it helped if one knew one looked at one's best.

They were the first to arrive, and were welcomed effusively by Mrs Hurley and rather more brusquely by Mr Hurley, the banker. Their son, George, made an elaborate bow over

Camilla's hand, continuing to hold on to it after he straightened up and pulled her a little closer. 'You're looking . . . er . . . rather magnificent this evening, Camilla. That's just the right colour for you, and what a pretty pendant!'

He peered more closely at the pendant, but Camilla knew where his eyes were really focussed and she pulled away sharply. 'Really, George! You are doing it a bit too brown tonight, are you not?' she reproved him. 'Besides, you have seen me in this gown before and made no such comment.'

'Didn't know I was supposed to.' George grinned. 'Dorothea's been giving me some hints, have you not, sis?' His sister was standing next in line and he nudged her arm. 'She said that you girls like to receive compliments so I practised a few. What d'you think, eh?'

'You can only get better, George,' Camilla said sweetly, moving on to be greeted by his sister. Miss Hurley was a few years older than Camilla and her small group of friends, and they met only on social occasions such as this. The two young ladies bobbed a slight curtsey to each other.

'I hope you won't feel under-dressed, Miss Brentwood,' Miss Hurley remarked, glancing down at her own frilled and flounced gown of pale pink silk. Her neck was adorned with a heavy arrangement of pink pearls, and a cluster of small pearls hung from each earlobe. 'Mama thought she and I ought to dress more finely, since we are the hostesses.'

Camilla privately thought Dorothea very over-dressed for a small informal dinner party. 'Who else is coming?' she asked, for something to say.

'Just Lord Westlake. Mama felt it appropriate to keep his first introduction to Kelsham society quite small. More select, don't you think?'

'Very select,' Camilla commented dryly. So, the young people were George, Miss Hurley, Lord Westlake and herself. She needed no crystal ball to foresee who would be seated next to whom!

George, still standing by her side, had obviously followed her train of thought. 'You will be happy to know I am to lead you in to dinner, Camilla. Wonder what this fellow looks like, hey? According to Father, he lacks a bit of town bronze.' He nudged her arm suggestively as he added, 'But plenty of town gold, hey!' He laughed at his own joke. 'I wouldn't mind a bit of that! Lucky fellow, being born son of a lord . . . even if he was a banished one! Wonder what his life has been like until now?'

'It is really none of our business,' Camilla protested, forgetting for a moment that she intended to have nothing to do with the interloper. Here she was, protecting his right to privacy!

'No, but one cannot help wondering, can one? One hears such outrageous tales from those who have been to the Americas! They live like savages, compared to us. No doubt he will need a lot of help in coping with the niceties of society.' He touched the folds of his cravat. 'I expect he will be glad of advice from a fellow like me. I shall take him around town and introduce him to one or two of my clubs.'

'You would do better encouraging him to come along to the Assemblies!' Dorothea criticised. 'We could suggest we make up a party next Wednesday. What do you say, Miss Brentwood? I'm sure George would be willing to escort you, wouldn't you, George?'

'Be more than happy to, m'dear!' George agreed with alacrity. He licked his lips as he looked at Camilla. 'Pity we are not having dancing later. Mother thought our party too small for that. But we can be partners for charades, can we not?'

Before Camilla could think of a suitable negative reply, the butler flung wide the doors and announced, 'Lord Westlake!'

All conversation ceased and seven pairs of eyes swung towards Lord Westlake, framed in the doorway. He was dressed in black pantaloons and a black evening jacket with satin reveres.

At his neck, a neat cravat fell in modest folds over his pristine white silk shirt. The cravat was held by a simple pin with a stone of black onyx. Camilla felt a lurch deep within her and her breath caught in her throat. Whatever was the matter with her? She knew the answer; Lord Westlake looked even more handsome than he had done in their previous encounters.

Across the room, his eyes met Camilla's and a light of recognition in their blue depths caused a strange breathlessness to flutter in her breast. Unknowingly, the tiny pink tip of her tongue parted her lips and withdrew again, leaving her lips moistened and still slightly apart. She felt suspended in the grip of timelessness, though she was aware that Mrs Hurley was sailing majestically forward towards her guest of honour.

'Lord Westlake! Welcome, my dear boy!' Mrs Hurley enthused, dropping into a wobbly curtsey at his feet. Banker Hurley had followed in her wake and now assisted her to rise as Lord Westlake made a courtly bow. Mr Hurley performed the introductions and Jack murmured how pleased he was to be there.

His eyes had at once lighted upon his little firebrand, as he had been thinking of her, and the light of recognition had sparked before he remembered that they had not officially met. Unconsciously, he glanced that way again and he felt Mrs Hurley tapping his arm with her folded fan, her plump face wreathed in a beaming smile.

'Ah, I see you have spotted the young ladies and want to meet them, you naughty boy!' she teased. 'Well, I won't keep you from them. They are as anxious to meet you as you are to meet them. Come, Dorothea! Come and make your curtsey to Lord Westlake. He is eager to make your acquaintance. Here she is, my lord. Our daughter, Dorothea.'

Dorothea sank into a curtsey, her frills and flounces billowing out around her. Jack couldn't help but think that she resembled a wobbly pink blanc-mange and was hard-pressed to keep his expression from betraying his thoughts.

'Miss Hurley,' he murmured, making his bow and schooling his features into a sober expression.

'And our son, George, named after our dear king! Of course, coming from America, you will find it strange that we honour our royal family so . . . but we shall soon teach you our ways, m'lord!' she added, once more flirtatiously tapping his arm with her fan.

He and George bowed stiffly. Jack nodded curtly, thinking how much George resembled the rotund Regent to whom he had been presented during his time in London, but merely murmured, 'Pleased to meet you.' He managed to keep his face impassive, though he detected a supercilious twist to the other fellow's mouth.

'And you, old boy!' George returned. 'Be glad to show you around your estate any time that's convenient.'

Jack raised an eyebrow. 'My grandfather's agent has already made arrangements, but I thank you for your offer.'

He moved on and was introduced to Arthur Brentwood and his wife, both of whom responded courteously to his bow.

'Of course, the Brentwoods have a son who might have been here tonight, but he is, at present, convalescing from injuries sustained on the Peninsula. Our soldiers are so brave, do you not think? And look so romantic in their uniform! He would have added quite a dash to our gathering.' Mrs Hurley chattered on garrulously. 'But then I would have had to invite another lady, which would have meant inviting the vicar and his wife and daughter . . . and then the Houghtons might have felt left out. And they have a son and two daughters, which would have meant . . . '

Her voice prattled on but Jack was not listening. His eyes met Miss Brentwood's and he could sense the hidden laughter that was barely being held in check. His eyes dropped to her perfectly shaped mouth, and he found himself wondering how it would feel to claim those lips with his own.

'And this is . . . ?' he queried.

Mrs Hurley was still in full lament over the difficulties in having a balanced table to dinner and it was Mrs Brentwood who took it upon herself to make the introduction. 'This is our daughter, m'lord,' she said somewhat wryly, making Jack think that she must have heard of their previous meeting.

He held Camilla's gaze, took hold of her hand and bowed over it as she bobbed a short but perfectly adequate curtsey. 'I am delighted to make your acquaintance, Miss Brentwood,' he said, noticing by the quick toss of her head that she had picked up on his reference to their previous meeting. Holding back laughter, he couldn't resist adding, 'I hear you like riding, Miss Brentwood? My butler tells me that you have been used to the freedom of riding on my land. Please feel free to continue to do so. I will instruct my men to ensure that your privacy is respected.'

'Thank you, m'lord!' she responded somewhat tersely, pulling her hand free of his light grip.

'Hey, we could make up a riding party, could we not?' George suggested, rubbing his hands together. 'How about tomorrow?'

Before Jack could remind George that he had already refused such an offer, Mrs Hurley, aware at last that the conversation had moved out of her control, said sharply, 'Now, George, dear, think of your sister!' She turned aside to Jack. 'Dorothea prefers the more gentle sport of carriage-riding, don't you, dear? So much more ladylike,' she added, drawing Dorothea back into the group.

Camilla, smarting from Lord Westlake's poking fun at her blunder of the other day, had no intention of being inveigled into an outing with him — neither on horseback, nor in a carriage.

'You are forgetting, George,' she said sweetly, flashing a smile his way, 'you had agreed to drive me into town tomorrow afternoon. We are meeting Susannah and the Houghtons at the Assembly Rooms. Do you not remember?' she prompted him, nodding her head vigorously.

'What? Did I?' He looked bewildered, as well he might, since he had made no such agreement. However he knew a good offer when he heard one. 'Oh, yes — so I did. Sorry, old chap. It will have to be another time.'

'Well, never mind, m'lord! Another day, perhaps?' Mrs Hurley consoled her guest, grateful at least that that minx had shown his lordship her preference for her son. If that liaison could be cemented, it would be one fewer setting her cap at his lordship — and that could only be favourable for her Dorothea!

'Dinner is ready to be served!' the Hurleys' butler announced loudly from the doorway.

Swiftly, Mrs Hurley organised the procession, bestowing a glowing Dorothea onto his lordship's arm. 'I know it should be I whom you lead in, m'lord, but Mr Hurley is more used to my uncertainty of balance. But, come, m'lord. I am so looking forward to hearing how you fared among all the savages in America. It must be so refreshing to now be in our civilised country among more refined people!'

*That'll show him!* Camilla grinned to herself as Dorothea clamped her hand on Lord Westlake's arm. So she was amazed when, in passing, Lord Westlake bent his head and whispered, 'Thank you. I am in your debt,' into her ear. Surely he did not want to have his name linked with Dorothea so soon after his arrival? He might find he was drawn into an unbreakable bond. Or did he consider a banker's daughter a good catch?

For some reason, that idea wasn't as appealing as she might have hoped.

# 5

You've agreed to go on a carriage drive this afternoon with George?' Susannah asked in amazement when Camilla called at the vicarage to report on the previous evening's dinner party. 'But you have always proclaimed that anyone who rides with George rides at their own peril!'

'Well, at the time, it seemed as though I was being manoeuvred into either horse-riding or a carriage drive with his lordship — so I quickly invented a previously arranged carriage drive with George. But, when his lordship later whispered that he was in my debt, I wondered if he saw my move as an opening for him to invite Dorothea to go for a carriage drive with him. He looked pretty pleased with himself as he led her into dinner!'

'Hmm. Maybe he sees her as an advantageous match? You know, money marrying money?' Susannah suggested.

'I am sure that is Mrs Hurley's aim; I seem to have inadvertently helped her. I wager Dorothea will be bowling along in style this afternoon, whilst I will be gripping the sides of my seat in danger of being thrown into a ditch!'

Which was exactly what Camilla was doing, a few hours later on their return from town. As they left the town behind them, Lord Westlake had just skimmed his way past them, nodding his head in their direction as he controlled his high-stepping pair with a light hand. The pace of his horses left them standing and, although George tried to whip his pair into a faster gait, the new lord and his bang-up-to-date sporting curricle had gone from their sight in a matter of seconds.

'And you say I drive too fast!' he glowered, his face a picture of envy.

'He has a very good hand,' Camilla couldn't help remarking. 'Did you notice the smooth line he kept on the bend?'

'Anyone can drive well if he has the money to buy a crack-up team!' George said petulantly. 'I would drive just as well with a set-up like that!'

'Yes, I am sure you would,' Camilla soothed him. 'However, I much prefer a gentler pace myself and I would appreciate it if you slowed down a little, George. We'll never catch him up, and your horses will be in a lather of sweat if you push them any further.'

Reluctantly George complied with her wishes, but his temper remained ruffled and Camilla was relieved to arrive home in one piece, wondering with a disturbing amount of pique if Lord Westlake was returning from an outing with Dorothea. No doubt the town would soon be agog with the news if, indeed, it proved to be the case!

The following day was Sunday. The Reverend Philip Yardley might have been forgiven for thinking that a revival of Pentecostal magnitude was sweeping the land, had not the earlier excited deliberations of his two daughters over what to wear to church alerted him to the fact that his parishioners would be attending that day's services with more of an eye towards the new Lord Westlake than to his modest sermon.

If Lord Westlake was aware of the avid interest in the details of his attire, every movement of his head and the fervour of his singing, he gave no sign. It was later agreed that his demeanour was extremely pleasant; his attire exactly as it should be for a lord of the realm; and his manner and personality exemplary.

For his part, Jack was happy to have made his first public appearance. He was glad to see that Ralph Brentwood was well enough to be present, though he walked with a slight limp and held his upper body carefully. He seemed to be friendly with the vicar's son, William, and the local magistrate's son, Lionel Houghton. He determined to make their various acquaintances within the next few days. As for George Hurley, his manner towards Miss

Brentwood seemed boorish and over-familiar. Or was there an 'understanding' between them that gave him the right to behave in such a familiar way? He had much to learn about his new neighbours, he realised.

Two days of inclement June weather kept him dealing with the business side of his affairs. A further meeting with his new bank manager completed the formalities of opening his new account, but did nothing to advance the banker in his estimation.

'You've got to know the right people, man!' Hurley boomed at him. 'I will be only too happy to sponsor you to the Gentlemen's Clubs. Someone plump in the pocket like you will find a warm welcome, I am sure! We might not rival White's of London but we are not so provincial that we cannot enjoy a wager or two! What d'you say, eh?'

So, the banker frequented the gaming tables, did he? It would be interesting to discover how restrained or liberal his gambling might be. Jack eyed him impassively. 'Civil of you, Hurley,' he murmured non-committally. 'I shall let you know if and when I require an introduction.'

Wednesday was bright and sunny. Good! Just the day to further his getting to know the layout of the estate and visit some of the farms.

By late morning, his circular journey was bringing him back to the vicinity of his home. The Avon flowed through his estate at this point and the flat meadowland along its banks enticed him to a fast gallop. He had just given Jupiter his head when a scream sounded from the direction of the river.

As his mind recollected that there was a weir around the curve of the river, just upriver from where he was, he heard an answering shout — a female voice. He gave a slight tug at his right-hand rein and pressed his knees into Jupiter's sides, spurring him into lengthening his stride. There wasn't time to ride around the hedgerow ahead, so he urged Jupiter straight at it, taking the leap in his stride.

Ahead, he could see a boy balancing precariously on the top of the weir. A chestnut horse was grazing on the near bank. He frowned. Surely it was the one Miss Brentwood had been riding on their first meeting! Had it been her cry he had heard? His gaze darted back to the river, where he could now see a clump of golden material billowing in the turbulent water at the foot of the weir. With a sense of shock, he realised that it was a woman's garment, and that its wearer was struggling to remain afloat without being swept downstream by the strong current. He realised that she was clutching a small limp form to her body.

At that moment, the boy on the weir tottered, lost his balance and, with a cry of alarm, tumbled down the stony side of the weir and disappeared into the foaming water at its foot, not far from the young woman. The boy surfaced a few yards from her and Jack could sense the woman's dilemma. Should she concentrate on the child in her grasp or attempt to grab him also? She did the latter. Had she no thought for her own safety?

'Hang on! I'm coming!' he yelled. They were being swept downstream towards him. He leaped off Jupiter, dragging off his coat as he ran to the bank. There, he jerked off his boots and plunged headlong into the water.

His shallow dive had taken him well away from the bank and he at once struck out for the figures he could just make out ahead of him. The current was swiftly bringing the trio within reaching distance.

'Keep hold of them!' he shouted, treading water as he shook the river water out of his eyes. 'I am going to tow all three of you to the bank. Don't struggle or you may have us all under water.'

The woman turned her head in the direction of his voice. It was indeed Miss Brentwood. Her dark hair was plastered to her head and her face showed the effects of her exertion.

'Have you got them secure?'

'Yes, I have!'

'Good! I am going to come behind you and take hold of you under your arms. If we kick together we should be able to get them to the bank.'

He did as he had said and, lying back in the water, he began the long struggle back to the bank. They had been carried more than a hundred yards downstream, where thankfully the current was becoming weaker. He realised that Miss Brentwood was matching his leg-stroke but, even so, she and the two children were a heavy burden to drag through the water.

'Nearly there!' he gasped in her ear. He let go of Miss Brentwood with one hand and grabbed at some overhanging branches. His feet were on the rocky riverbed and he pulled himself upright, dragging the trio closer to the bank. He grasped the boy's arm. 'Let go of this child and grab this branch.'

He took the boy out of her arms and

heaved him onto the grassy bank, where the lad immediately began to retch up some water. That was a good sign. He hurriedly reached for the other child — a girl, he realised, as she lay limply in his arms. He quickly placed her face down on the bank and then hauled Miss Brentwood upright and hustled her up the banking, where she flopped in exhaustion, dragging air into her lungs in rasping breaths. He patted her back heartily, uttering tersely, 'You'll live!'

He turned his attention to the small girl, thankful for his grandfather's belief that all boys should learn practical survival skills. He had seen more than one life saved from a probable drowning by having the water pumped out of the victim's system. After a few moments, the girl began to retch and splutter, coughing up river water.

'Ah! Thank the Lord!'

He realised Miss Brentwood was kneeling at his side. The heat of the sun was creating clouds of steam from their wet garments, yet all four of them were shivering.

'Will she recover?' she asked urgently.

'I think so. Though the fact that she is very thin and undernourished will not help. She needs to be put into dry clothing as soon as possible. As do you, Miss Brentwood.'

He had noticed that her teeth were chattering uncontrollably and he stood up, holding out a hand to draw her to her feet. 'Your prompt action saved these two children from drowning — but I feel compelled to point out that had I not chanced along this way, all three of you might have perished in the river. Your action was, perhaps, a little foolhardy.'

'Really?' Miss Brentwood's voice lost its easy warmth and her eyebrows rose perceptibly. 'You would have had me remain on the river bank wringing my hands, perhaps? Or should I have made my groom risk his life when he cannot swim, instead of sending him off to get help?'

'Your groom was with you?'

'Of course!' Her eyes suddenly narrowed. 'Or are you, perhaps, suggesting that the lives of two village children are of less importance than mine?' She looked more closely at the two children huddled together, the girl sobbing for her mother and the boy doing his unsuccessful best to comfort her. 'You are Tommy Dutton, are you not?' she asked. 'And this is your sister Mary? Is your elder sister Dora still employed at the Hall?'

'Yes, she is, miss.'

'They are children of your tenants, Lord Westlake. You have responsibility for them. As for being thin and undernourished, that is not their fault, nor the fault of their parents. Many farmers around here suffered bad harvests last year. There has been no one here to help your tenants. Many are in great financial difficulties — but not to the extent that they would rather their children drown in the river to relieve them of the burden of feeding them!'

Jack held out his hands, palms forward, as if warding off her wrath.

'No, no, Miss Brentwood! I meant no such thing. I was merely making an observation that you had, unthinkingly, put yourself in grave danger.'

Why had he started this? It had been a moment of misplaced concern for a fragility Miss Brentwood did not possess.

'As you did for me?' she now countered.

'Ah, yes — but I am a man and have swum in rougher waters than these.'

'And I have swum in these very waters, Lord Westlake — though not in such voluminous clothing.' She glanced down at her sodden attire, only now realising how it clung to her body, revealing her curves. She bit her lower lip and then tossed back her head, a defiant glint in her eyes. 'I would have been less hampered in breeches and jacket!'

Jack inclined his head in wry agreement. He tore his gaze away from her shapely figure and tried to push from his memory the feel of her soft body as he had held her against him and manhandled her out of the river . . . but the blush suffusing her face revealed how transparent his thoughts had been.

To cover his less than gallant thoughts, he added hastily, 'Let us argue no further. I spoke only from concern for your safety and I am heartily glad you rescued the children. But you are shivering. We need to get you somewhere warm.' He placed two fingers in his mouth, emitting a shrill whistle. An answering whinny told him that Jupiter was on his way and, trotting in his wake, came Miss Brentwood's chestnut.

'Cor, Mister!' Tommy breathed in admiration. He reached out reverently to touch the stallion as he came to an obedient halt by his master's side, nuzzling against his neck.

'Do you feel able to ride, Miss Brentwood?' Jack asked her.

'Of course!'

He cupped his hands to receive her sodden booted foot and threw her up easily into the saddle — a lady's side-saddle this time. 'Will you take the girl? Can you manage her?'

'As long as she sits still. And she is called Mary. Hand her to me.'

'Am I riding wi' you, Mister?' Tommy asked in awed tones as Jack handed his sister to Miss Brentwood.

'You are, lad.'

'Cor!' The boy's face shone with excitement.

'He is Lord Westlake, not 'Mister', Tommy,' Camilla quietly reproved him, as Jack walked the few yards to collect his boots and jacket; the latter of which he draped around her shoulders on his return.

'Thank you, but do go on ahead, Lord Westlake. We are on your land, and there is no danger of my losing my way. You could be alerting your staff to our needs and possibly sending a message to Mr and Mrs Dutton,' she added sensibly. 'Your housekeeper might be appreciative of the chance to have preparations under way before we get there. I will follow with Mary at my own pace and will be with you shortly.'

That made sense. He agreed to her suggestion and, to Tommy's delight, they covered the remaining distance in no time at all, meeting a couple of his newly-hired stable-hands running towards the river with Miss Brentwood's groom in their wake. He handed over the lad and swiftly gave orders to them to alert his housekeeper before whirling Jupiter around and galloping back to relieve Miss Brentwood of her burden.

Back at the Hall, he found that Mrs Winslade had swiftly organised her diminished staff into replenishing the hot-water boiler normally reserved for laundry days and had put aside her sitting-room for Miss Brentwood's use.

'I have sent for Dr Morris, m'lord,' she informed him, as she took the shivering but calm child out of his arms. 'And I have sent word to the

Brentwoods. I am sure someone will be here as soon as they can.'

Jack thanked her and assisted Miss Brentwood to dismount.

Despite her assurances that she was 'Fine, just fine! Really I am,' she almost stumbled against him as her feet touched the cobbled yard and he could tell that the unexpected river rescue had taken its toll.

He was thankful to hand her into Mrs Winslade's care whilst he retired to his own quarters to shed his own wet clothes and receive a brisk rubbing down in a tub of hot water. Once dressed again, he settled down in his library with a warming glass of brandy, confident that he had done all that was necessary.

When he later heard the front door bell peal, he assumed it was either the doctor or Mrs Brentwood come to take care of her daughter. He discovered his error when he emerged from the library to give his welcome.

The doctor was indeed at the top of

the steps but, close on his heels, was the figure of Mrs Hurley, her expression avid with curiosity. Even as he moved forward to attempt to dissuade her from her untimely visit, he saw her expression change to one of gleeful shock and her exclamation of 'Miss Brentwood!' told him the reason why.

Jack turned his head to follow Mrs Hurley's line of vision. Miss Brentwood, her slim figure inelegantly wrapped around in one of Mrs Winslade's oversized gowns, had entered the hallway from the direction of the kitchen. He would have burst out laughing had the situation not been quite so potentially damaging to Miss Brentwood's reputation.

Camilla's eyes widened with dismay.

# 6

Later that day when they were returned to Greenacres, Eleanor reproached her daughter. 'Oh, Camilla! How could you appear in Lord Westlake's company dressed in such a manner? To think it was Violet Hurley who saw you! She will have the tale around the district before the day is out.'

'I don't think so, Mama.' Camilla smiled. 'I told her I had no intention of depriving the other young ladies in the district of their chance to catch the most eligible parti of the year! You should have seen the calculating expression that swept over her face as the implication of what I was saying sank in. She had to choose between being the bearer of scandalous gossip — gossip that would have denied Dorothea her chance of 'catching' Lord Westlake for herself — or accepting our word that nothing improper had taken place, and that I had been in Mrs Winslade's company until that moment. She chose the latter, and promised to say no more about it.'

'And what did Westlake himself make of your declaration? I hope you did not hurt his feelings.'

'I believe I did not. He did offer to stand by propriety and make me 'respectable', but I told him not to be such a flat as I considered myself to be respectable enough without his aid — and added that I had no intention of entrapping him. I am sure he was much relieved by my refusal.'

'Very likely,' Eleanor agreed. 'We must visit the Duttons tomorrow to make sure that the children are recovered from their ordeal. I shall ask Cook to make some suitable food for the family — though I have no doubt that Mrs Winslade will have sent them home with something.'

She was correct in that respect. When Camilla and her mother visited Dutton's farm the following afternoon, Mrs Dutton was full of praise for the new Lord Westlake.

'He came 'imself, ma'am,' she said in awed tones. 'Brought 'em 'ome wi' our Dora, 'e did . . . and a large piece of' 'am and a basket o' vegetables . . . and he insisted that our Dora stayed overnight in case either of the two little 'uns took bad in the night. I've sent 'er back this mornin', though. I didn't want to tek advantage o' his good nature. Eeh, 'e teks after his grandfather, 'e does an' all! Said as 'e'll get Pickford to come around and sort out some repairs. I could 'ave cried with relief. And 'e said 'e'll take our Tommy on in 'is stables.'

'Well, that is a piece of good news, is it not, Camilla?' Eleanor agreed. 'All we need now is a good harvest this year . . . not like last year's disaster.'

'And 'e said as 'e'll make sure we get 'elp with that!' Mrs Dutton continued, nodding her head vigorously, her lean face shining with pleasure. 'An' 'e said as 'ow it was you, Miss Brentwood, what really saved our Tommy an' Mary from the river. I can't thank 'ee enough for that, Miss.'

'I was just thankful to be in a position to help them, Mrs Dutton,' Camilla assured her, pleasurably surprised by all that Lord Westlake had already achieved. And he seemed to have taken some of her words to heart. She smiled at Mrs Dutton. 'I am sure Lord Westlake will do all that is necessary to help you and all his other tenants get back on your feet.'

And to her own surprise, she fully believed what she said.

When they returned home, Norris, their butler, informed them that they had missed a visitor. 'Lord Westlake, Ma'am. Mr Ralph received him in his suite and he departed not ten minutes since.'

Camilla found herself eager to hear what Lord Westlake had had to say but managed to present no more than a cool interest when Ralph recounted part of their conversation.

'He is a very nice chap, Camilla. You should be more lenient towards him. Not his fault he has inherited the estate, and he intends to do his duty by it.' He raised an eyebrow towards his sister, adding, 'Someone seems to have informed him that many of his tenants are in a bad way financially.'

Camilla felt a guilty flush rising over her cheeks. 'Someone needed to do so. There's talk that Mr Hurley is about to foreclose on some loans. Old Lord Westlake would turn in his grave if any of his tenants got turned off their farms!'

'It is his land agent's job to do that, Camilla. Not yours.'

Camilla tossed her head. 'Well, if that is so, why had Pickford not told him? He's surely had enough time to do so.'

Which was exactly what Jack was, at that very moment, demanding of his land agent.

Pickford shifted his stance, uncomfortably aware that the young lord had somehow discovered information that he himself had neglected to bring to his notice.

'I thought you would need more time to gain an overall impression of the estates, m'lord,' he mumbled, 'before having to make any decisions that might prove rather unpopular with some of your tenants.'

'I am sure nothing could make me more unpopular than my having to stand by whilst the bank foreclosed on their loans and deprived them of their livelihood, man!' Jack pointed out with restraint. 'What I find unbelievable is that it was you who advised them to take that course of action. Surely the estate should have taken care of any such need. Or didn't my grandfather care what happened to his tenants?'

'He was old, m'lord. It was all getting too much for him,' Pickford protested weakly.

'But was that not why he employed a land agent? Was it not your job to bring such things to his attention, Pickford, and advise him what to do?'

'He was a barmy old . . . that is, his mind was going, m'lord. He wouldn't listen. Then he died, and everything was tied up. Mr Timothy had no authority . . . and nobody knew about you, milord. Mr Hurley offered to step in and underwrite the losses. It seemed a good idea at the time, with it being uncertain how long it would be before his lordship's heir was discovered.' He shifted uneasily, hoping his lordship did not also know about the cash-in-hand he received from the banker for each such recommendation.

Jack was not impressed, either by his land agent's explanation or his own dealings with the bank. He drummed his fingertips on the desk as he pondered what to do. Could he trust Pickford if he allowed him to continue working for him? He looked at the man standing anxiously before him and decided to leave things be for the moment.

'I will be looking into everything closely over the next few days, Pickford,' he warned. 'If you have any misgivings over continuing to work for me, tell me now and we will bring your employment here to an end. No? Then I shall expect total honesty and loyalty from you in the future. Is that clear?'

'Yes, m'lord.'

'Good. And I do not want any mention of what we have been discussing to leave this room. Is that also clear?'

'Yes, m'lord.'

'Good. Your first task is to draw up a list of each one of my tenants who has taken out a loan from Mr Hurley's bank — or indeed, any other bank — and I want that list before you finish work for today. You may go.'

Pickford turned to leave but halted when Jack spoke again.

'And, Pickford, I do not want to find out that you have been in contact with Mr Hurley or any other banker before I have had the opportunity to sort this business out.'

Pickford hesitated, but the steadiness of his employer's gaze gave him no leeway. After a moment, he mumbled, 'No, m'lord,' and left the room.

Jack hoped he had done the right thing. At least, from now on, he would be keeping a close eye on Pickford — and better the dog you know than the one you don't. His fingertips drummed again. His own people, he could help — but he could not help suspecting that Josiah Hurley might be overstepping his rightful financial dealings with many more local businesses. He wondered how he might help them also.

★ ★ ★

He presented himself at Hurley's bank at five minutes past ten the following morning. The clerk leapt to his feet and scurried into the inner office before Jack had time to take his hat off. He reappeared in less than a minute with the bank manager close on his heels.

Mr Hurley beamed, rubbing his hands together as if already anticipating more money coming into them. 'Good morning, Lord Westlake. And what can we do for you this fine morning? More business, eh? Can't keep a good man away from his money, what!'

Jack had already decided to underplay both his knowledge and his level of intelligence. He returned the greeting, twirling his right hand in the air, gesturing in the general direction of the inner office. 'A few moments of your time, Hurley? Need to clarify a few things, you know.'

'My time is at your disposal, sir,' Hurley said grandly, standing back and indicating for Jack to precede him into the office. 'Never too busy to see a customer such as yourself, m'lord! A pleasure to have you in my establishment. Do take a seat.'

Jack seated himself and languidly crossed his right leg over his other knee. 'Seems I owe you some gratitude, sir, for easing the lot of some of my tenants last year. Most handsome of you. You should have let me know I was indebted to you when we last met. I would have cleared the loans immediately. My grandpappy used to say, 'Never let the sun set upon a debt!' Still, no harm done, eh?'

He was amused to see the various expressions flit across the banker's face — bewilderment, dawning understanding, suspicion and distinct annoyance. 'Your tenants, m'lord? Have they complained to you? The transactions were perfectly legal, I assure you!'

'No, no! No complaints, Hurley. Just my lackadaisical land agent finally doing his duty when some details were innocently leaked to me. Knew immediately what I had to do. Can't have one's tenants keeping their master afloat, eh? Not done . . . not in my grandpappy's view, anyway!'

'Just so, m'lord,' Hurley ground out. 'Exactly which of these debts have you in mind?'

'All of them, of course.' Jack twirled his hand again. 'Can't settle one and not the rest, can I? Drew up a list.' He fished inside the inner pocket of his jacket and withdrew a slim folded paper. 'I think you'll find them all there — and just in time for some of them, eh!' He uttered this latter remark as if it would come as good news to Hurley, and laughed inwardly as the banker strove to twist his furious glare into what might pass for an agreeable smile.

'Hmm! Of course, you realise that these amounts exceed the amount deposited in your account in this bank, m'lord,' Hurley pointed out, a note of hopeful expectancy in his voice.

'Ah! I knew you would soon spot that!' Jack said, as if in admiration of the banker's astuteness. 'What I propose is, as one gentleman to another, I will take over these debts and take out a new, short-term loan with you that will be settled as soon as my London banker forwards a draft to cover the whole amount.' He beamed at Hurley. 'I deal with Coutts — a most prominent banker, you will agree. Of course, I will make sure that he hears of your generous spirit and I am sure he will advise me to review my meagre dealing with you.'

He saw Josiah Hurley swallow hard, his eyes swiftly shifting from side to side as he weighed up possible advantages to himself and his own bank in this new deal. Jack leaned back in his seat, giving the impression of total ease over the outcome of Hurley's hasty deliberations.

The banker's hope for an increase of business from Lord Westlake won over any misgivings. He slapped his hand onto his desk. 'You have a deal, m'lord! I will get my clerk to draw up the details forthwith and have it ready for you tomorrow.'

'Excellent!' Jack smiled. He rose to his feet and inclined his head. 'I have enjoyed doing business with you, Mr Hurley. Until tomorrow, then.'

\* \* \*

Once on the steps of the bank, Jack paused and looked up and down the main street, wondering how many of the businesses had fallen into Hurley's hands, their owners now struggling to keep abreast with paying off loans. From the rumours he had so far heard, it must be at least fifty per cent of them. It was time to put into action the plan he had discussed with Ralph Brentwood the previous day. He intended to join the various Gentlemen's Clubs — but not under the sponsorship of the banker. He and Ralph were about to go out on the town, sponsored instead by Arthur Brentwood.

'Not that you would need my sponsorship, Westlake, but it shows a pleasing sensibility in your character that you request it. I am more than happy to agree, m'lord.'

Consequently, Jack joined Ralph and Lionel Houghton, the magistrate's son, on a few rounds of the clubs, which, though not as well-known as their London counterparts, gave equal opportunities for their members to enjoy pitting their wits and nerve against Lady Luck.

Lionel and Ralph were steady players

who made neither spectacular gains nor losses. Initially, Jack showed himself to be a worthy opponent at card games that required a degree of skill, but to display indiscretion where 'chance' was the predominant factor. As the evening wore on, after consuming a fair amount of liquor, his skill became erratic and when the trio eventually left the tables that night, Jack had made more losses than wins.

The second time at the gaming tables followed the same pattern. George Hurley was at the table this time, and it seemed to the casual observer that Lord Westlake was allowing himself to be goaded into more reckless play by the banker's son's erratic stakes. George was the one who rose from the table with a hearty smile on his face.

'I'll give you the chance to win it back, Westlake,' he offered generously. He glanced around and, finding no one else near enough to overhear what he was saying, went on quietly, 'There is a rather exclusive club I could introduce you to. Only a select few, you understand. What d'you say, eh? Shall I approach my father on your behalf?'

Swaying slightly, Jack eagerly agreed. 'Just the ticket, old boy! That should liven things up.'

'Good. It should be arranged by Saturday. We'll go together, shall we?'

Jack agreed. He knew he was taking a risk, since the invitation was not extended to Ralph and Lionel, but he needed to learn more of Josiah Hurley's night-time activities. Hopefully, he would be able to lure the banker into making him the sort of indiscreet offer that he suspected he had forced upon others among his clients.

Jack was also making progress on the social front. Knowing that a keen eye was being kept on his actions by every 'mama' in the district, he was careful to spread his attentions among all the young ladies. He wanted to satisfy his social conscience first, and so he was in no hurry to settle his affections. Invitations to routs and balls and picnics came flooding in, and he was happy to accept the majority of them.

One such evening at a local ball, as he was leading Camilla onto the floor to join a set of the quadrille, a petulant voice was clearly heard to say, 'Of course, Miss Brentwood sent away the old lord's younger grandson when his expectations came to naught! It's obvious that she is now setting her cap at this one.'

Jack could tell that Miss Brentwood had heard the comment by the way a delightful pink colour flowed over her flawless countenance, though, apart from a brief tension in her otherwise lithe body, she gave no other sign of discomfort. As they progressed through the complicated moves of the dance, he glanced in the direction from where the remark had come but did not recognise any of the young ladies standing there.

However, when one of them later detached herself from the group and made her way to where Miss Hurley was standing, he suspected he knew the source — confirmed when that lady proceeded to exchange a series of whispers behind her fan, causing her confidante to smile in a satisfied way. He was not blind to Mrs Hurley's endeavours to thrust her daughter in his path and had felt sorry that the young woman was made to suffer the indignities of her mother's actions. Consequently, he realised, he had possibly given her hope to believe that his feelings for her were more deeply meant than he intended. Hmm. He had better back off from there!

He glanced at his partner and was taken by surprise at the sudden lurch of desire somewhere deep inside him. He shrugged it aside, though he doubted Miss Brentwood was seeking to entrap him. In fact, now he considered it, Miss Brentwood and her friend Miss Morris, the doctor's daughter, were the only two young ladies whom he had never had cause to think were out to engage his affections.

Miss Morris was clearly head-over-heels in love with young Houghton and the couple were, even at this moment, gazing starry-eyed at each other as they went through the motions of the dance. But, if anything, the main emotion he detected from his current partner was that of reserved resentment — and the alacrity with which she had distanced herself from his enforced offer to preserve her reputation after her river rescue showed she had no inclination to set her cap at him!

A pity, really. She was the only one of his present social set with whom he felt any rapport. He glanced across the set at her. Her face was set in a pleasant but impersonal smile that indicated she was still aware of critical eyes upon her.

Her eyes flickered to his and his immediate reaction was to smile openly at her. She held his gaze, and he saw her eyes initially widen slightly and then suddenly flood with wry amusement.

His own grin widened in appreciation of her acknowledgement of the constraints they were under and, without realising it, their steps momentarily halted as they simultaneously felt the impact of their shared moment.

Jack felt stunned as a shaft of something — he wasn't sure what — scorched through his body. It was only the movements of the other three couples in their set that made his feet automatically perform the steps they had learned. The moment was gone, but the memory of it remained, and he had no idea how he managed to complete the dance and return Miss Brentwood to her place by her mama and Mrs Morris, murmuring the correct pleasantries as he made his bow and took his leave of them.

He was not sure whether he was thankful or regretful that he had promised to make his debut at Loxton's Gaming Parlour later that evening. He just hoped that he could reclaim the cool head that he knew he needed if he were to succeed in discovering how Hurley had got so many local business-men into his financial clutches.

# 7

Camilla was in similar turmoil. She was not sure what had happened. One moment she was adequately performing the complicated steps of the quadrille; the next she was in a state of stunned stupor as she felt her gaze held by Lord Westlake's laughing eyes. Her chest had suddenly felt so constricted that she felt herself in danger of being unable to breathe and, surely, for a moment at least, she was sure her heart had stopped beating! A strange warmth had then spread around her body, enveloping her in a cloak of suppressed wonder, and it was only as her feet had resumed the pattern of steps that she felt a semblance of normal composure returning.

Lord Westlake gave no indication that he had been similarly stricken. She could only suppose that the remark she had overheard had upset her more than she had at first realised and that she had suffered some sort of delayed reaction to it. It was only as the dance ended and Lord Westlake had departed from the ballroom immediately after he had escorted her back to her mama that it occurred to her that instead of Lord Westlake laughing *with* her at that catty attack on her motives, he must have been laughing *at* her — and that he could barely wait to distance himself from her and the embarrassing situation he found himself in.

In response to her mama's anxious queries about her distracted air, she merely pleaded that the heat of the ballroom had fatigued her and she wished to sit out the next few dances. The fact that one of those dances was pledged to George Hurley and that he did not come to claim it only gave her a sense of relief; she was unaware that her missing partner had left the ballroom at the same time as Lord Westlake, and that they were now on their way to

Loxton's Gaming Hall where they intended to while away the rest of the evening.

Camilla schooled her features into a semblance of enjoyment but was thankful when at last the ball ended, and she was able to return to the sanctuary of her home and her own room. There, she submitted to the disrobing ministrations of her maid, but sleep did not come easily. Her thoughts were too disturbed by the memory of the strange sensation that had overcome her — and her later dismay at what she believed Lord Westlake's reaction to the remark had been.

How could she face him again if he believed her to be a fortune huntress in pursuit of a title?

★  ★  ★

It was Jack's fourth visit to Loxton's. On his previous three visits he had shown himself to be an indifferent player and it was quite easy for a seasoned gamester to anticipate his downfall. So far, he had made relatively small bets but had gradually increased the amounts of his wagers, giving the impression that his naturally conservative manner could be eroded with comparative ease.

Josiah Hurley had been present on two of his previous visits; the first, when Jack had caught sight of the banker sweating over the cards in his hands and eventually slinking away with a worried look upon his face; and on his third visit, when Hurley seemed to be having better luck and had eventually gathered his winnings together. Catching sight of Jack in the midst of an interested group, he had nodded affably to him. 'And how about you, m'lord? Do you fancy your chances at the table tonight? Though I must warn you that I am on a winning streak!'

Jack had languidly agreed to play. He was dealt indifferent hands, some of which he won, others he lost. He eventually declared he had lost enough for one night and made his farewells, promising to return another night to attempt to reverse his run of bad fortune.

This was the night. He played a few hands with George Hurley, losing a few hundred pounds to him, until Hurley senior appeared behind his son.

'Bad luck, m'lord!' he commiserated with geniality. 'Maybe a change of opponent will change your luck? Willing to give it a try, eh?'

Jack agreed, and father and son changed places. The first few games went either way but, as the stakes rose, Jack's recklessness increased, until he put his palms on the table and declared in slurred tones, 'That'sh it for tonight, Hurley. Musht quit whilst my dibs are still in tune!'

'Oh, I am ready to accept your note of hand, m'lord,' Hurley said, leaning back in his chair. 'Why not try another hand? A young fellow like you must know you win nothing without taking a risk! I always say you have to stake high to win high. Shall we double the last stake for a final round?'

Jack's gaze seemed a little unfocussed as he tried to look the banker in the eye. 'One more,' he agreed. 'Then really must go. Got to go to London tomorrow to see my man of business. Hic!'

The next game went the same way as the others and Jack slumped in his chair, aware that men around their table were watching with varying degrees of sympathy or antipathy. 'That'sh it! Almosht at point non plus! I'll write my note and shee you sometime tomorrow, Hurley. Musht go now!'

Jack staggered from the room and out of the Club, thankful that he had had the foresight to tell his groom to be waiting with his carriage. He sank back against the seat rest, hoping he hadn't gone too far with his gamble that night. He didn't believe in Lady Luck, but he certainly needed some form of a guardian angel watching over him!

The following day, he did not go to the bank until lunchtime. Then, with his demeanour more abashed than on previous occasions, he requested an interview with Mr Hurley.

The clerk smirked at him. 'Oh, he'll see you, right enough, m'lord. Told me to show you right in, he did.'

Hurley did not rise from his chair when Jack stepped into the inner office. He indicated that Jack take a seat and then leaned back, his fingers meeting tip to tip over his corpulent belly. He pursed his lips together and surveyed Jack's abject expression.

'Seems you went in a bit too deep last night, m'lord,' he remarked mildly. 'I suppose you have funds in your London bank to back you up?'

Jack looked disconcerted. 'Not as much as I would have hoped, Hurley. Should not have emptied my basket settling my tenants' affairs! Got a right rollicking from London over that, I can tell you.' He made an affected laugh. 'I took a gamble on being able to get back on level ground and no-one being any the wiser!'

'Indeed! I had no idea!' Hurley said in genuine surprise. 'Course, the old man kept his affairs close to his chest. Well, well, well!'

He tapped the tips of his fingers together, apparently lost in thought, then clasped his hands together in a decisive manner. 'As it happens, m'lord, I may be able to help you out here. It just so happens that I have got inside knowledge of a new venture and have been wondering which of my clients I might approach in order to offer them the chance to make a sure profit. Of course, my bank could underwrite the whole venture; but I have decided to take up only fifty per cent of it myself and share out the other fifty among my favoured clients.'

He opened a drawer in his desk, took out a sheaf of papers and handed the top sheet to Jack. 'Here's the name of the Company and a summary of the details.'

Jack quickly scanned his eyes over the paper, taking in the name of the proposed business and as much as he could of the details.

Hurley narrowed his eyes at Jack. 'Would you be interested, m'lord? It would solve your immediate problem and set you up in good balance for the future, though I must warn you that all investments carry an amount of risk. But I need a quick answer, you understand. A good venture like this doesn't stay open for long. There will be others who will want a cut themselves.'

Jack returned the paper in a bored manner, stifling a yawn. 'It sounds capital, Hurley,' he drawled. 'I am most grateful to you, sir. How soon can you draw up the papers?'

Hurley leaned forward and said conspiratorially, 'I presume your visit to London is to visit your other banker in person, is it? Of course, as I said on your first visit, it would be much simpler if you were to deposit all your money here, m'lord.'

'You could be right, Hurley. You could be right,' Jack agreed with a nonchalant air.

'Very wise, sir. I will have papers drawn up regarding this venture and they will be ready on your return from London.' He rose from his chair and moved towards the door, showing that the interview was over. 'Until your return, then, m'lord.'

Jack departed, glad to be out in the open again. He trusted that his trip to London would prove to be as informative as he hoped.

★ ★ ★

'Westlake's scarpered to London!' announced George Hurley gleefully to the group of young people at the Assembly Rooms the following day. 'He took quite a thrashing at the gaming tables the other night. Seemed to think he was in dun territory!'

'What? Surely not! Do not be absurd, George,' Camilla said scathingly, shocked by the revelation. 'He'd have to lose a fortune to be at a standstill.' She turned agitatedly to her brother, whom she knew had accompanied Lord Westlake to the gentlemen's clubs on some occasions of late. 'Don't you agree, Ralph?'

Ralph shrugged. 'I was not with him last night, but he has been going for higher and higher stakes. However, I am sure he will be able to sort something out with his London bank.'

'He's a loser!' George crowed. 'I knew it would happen sooner or later. Like father, like son, I always say . . . and we all know what sort of fellow his father was.' He patted his pocket, adding, 'Anyway, every cloud has a silver lining. I made quite a killing! Just wait until I get the new racing curricle I have ordered. That will show Lord High-and-Mighty that he is not the only one who can cut a dash. If he comes back, that is.'

Camilla felt truly shaken. She was still uncertain about her feelings towards Lord Westlake, but she had begun to allow her heart to respond to the easy rapport that seemed to exist between them — though the manner of his leaving her still rankled. She turned to her brother again. 'Could he really be so rolled up that he could be in financial trouble?'

'I was there when he gave my father his note of hand,' George put in, relishing his chance to discredit the new lord. 'And his funds in my father's bank could not match it.'

'It is not our place to speculate about Lord Westlake's monetary affairs,' Ralph cautioned. 'It's not the done thing, old chap.'

'Maybe not. But I say it will bring him down a peg or two,' George smirked in response. 'Rags to riches and back again! Wait till you see my new curricle, Cammy. It's bang up to the nines. Promise me you will be the first to ride in it.'

Feeling distracted by her disappointment over Lord Westlake's fall from grace and his subsequent removal to the capital, Camilla absently murmured her agreement. Huh! So much for thinking Lord Westlake was going to improve the lot of his tenants. He was more likely going to condemn them to further misery by his wasteful excesses!

★ ★ ★

In spite of Ralph's caution, Lord Westlake's departure to London gave rise to considerable speculation in the area, especially after rumours of his bout of reckless gambling began to spread around. Arthur Brentwood huffed his disappointment in the young man and Camilla found herself torn between agreeing with him and, for some unfathomable reason, wanting to defend him.

Her social calendar seemed to have lost its sparkle over the next few days. She had not realised how much she had begun to look for Lord Westlake's appearance at the various events, and now his continued absence took the sparkle out of every engagement.

Within a day or so, the gossip about Lord Westlake was pushed aside by the arrival in town of two seemingly unconnected men, neither of whom seemed distinctive in any way but who had taken up residence in the local inn and who seemed to spend much of the day quietly visiting the various businesses in town.

However, none of the owners of those businesses were communicative about what had actually been discussed and interest in the two strangers waned from lack of fuel, to be replaced by anticipation of the annual Garden Party that was to be held in the vicarage garden in a couple of weeks' time.

★ ★ ★

Finally, after an absence of just over a week, Lord Westlake was back. Camilla had been out riding and, on her return was informed by her maid that Lord Westlake was visiting and, having spent fifteen minutes in polite conversation with Mrs Brentwood, was now with Mr Ralph in the library.

Camilla strove to calm her racing heart. She allowed her maid to disrobe her from her riding habit and, after sponging her skin and tidying her hair, to assist her into a day gown of pale pink sprigged muslin. Camilla then paced back and forth in a fit of indecision, torn between wanting to know exactly what had happened and risking her dignity in being snubbed by his lordship's possible indifference to her.

After a moment, inspiration struck. She slipped out into the garden where she knew Andrews, their gardener, was weeding the perennial borders.

'I have a fancy to cut some roses, Andrews,' she said pleasantly.

'Right, miss. I shall get you a basket and some scissors.'

He got to his feet and ambled off to his shed, where the necessary items were kept, and took them to the rose garden, where Camilla was already examining the blooms. She couldn't help glancing towards the library window that overlooked this part of their grounds, but was unable to discern if either of its occupants was looking outside.

'Here you are, miss. There's a few good 'uns in that bed over there that are just about ready.'

'Thank you, Andrews.'

Camilla strolled to where Andrews had indicated and began to carefully select the budded roses, elegantly stretching for those just out of reach. Five minutes or more must have passed before she heard footsteps approaching, but she affected to be absorbed in her task until he spoke.

'I hope I find you well, Miss Brentwood.'

She turned as if startled. 'Oh, Lord Westlake! I see you are returned from your business in London.'

Jack bowed. 'I am indeed. May I hold your basket? Then you can reach the far roses more easily.'

His admiring gaze brought a faint

heat to Camilla's cheeks but she handed the basket to him, delighting in the tingling in her fingers as their hands briefly touched. She turned away quickly and reached for another rose stem.

'Was your visit to town successful?' she asked, trying to keep her voice from betraying the tremor within.

'Ah! Now that depends on what you suppose my purpose to have been.'

'I am sure it is no business of mine, Lord Westlake.'

Her voice sounded extremely prim, more so than she had intended. She was not surprised when Lord Westlake rejoined, 'Have I upset you, Miss Brentwood? I thought that we were becoming friends.'

Camilla decided to be honest with him. 'Yes . . . but I was a little hurt when you departed so abruptly from the Ellisons' ball. It made me think you had somehow been amused at my expense.'

Jack was surprised by her answer. He recalled the wonderful feeling of rapport he had felt that evening, the shaft of euphoria that had sped through his body. Then he also recalled the overheard slur on her character, and how soon he had left afterwards to go to Loxton's.

'Then I must apologise about my abrupt departure. Time had sped by that evening. I suddenly recollected an important engagement.'

'To go gambling,' Camilla returned coolly.

'Ah! Gossip has spread the news of my downfall? Again, I apologise.' He smiled disarmingly. 'It was a temporary aberration, Miss Brentwood. I have been . . . er . . . chastised over it by my man of business in London and I can promise you, I will take care not to repeat the error. At least, not in so extreme a fashion. I take it you will not mind if I have the occasional flutter?'

Camilla looked at him sharply and saw that his eyes were crinkled with laughter. She quickly turned away and snipped another rose. 'It is really no business of mine whatever you do, Lord

Westlake,' she answered.

'No,' he agreed calmly. He was enjoying the freedom in which they were bantering. 'But perhaps I am not averse to your concern over my affairs.' His eyebrow rose quizzically as he spoke and was charmed by the faint pink flush that crept once more over her cheeks.

Camilla felt confused. 'I am not sure I know what you mean, Lord Westlake,' she said, her tone belying the severity of her words. 'But I am willing to be . . . friends, if that is what you meant.'

Jack laughed, hearing the thawing tone of her voice. 'It is, Miss Brentwood, and I count myself favoured to be your friend. As your friend, then, may I suggest that you have cut quite enough roses for one day? I am sure your gardener will be quite distraught if he finds his carefully nurtured bushes stripped of all their blooms!'

Camilla glanced at the overfull trug. 'Oh!' She hadn't been aware that she had cut so many. 'You are quite right.

Oh no, my dress!' She looked in dismay at her dress, caught on some thorns.

Lord Westlake put down the basket and stepped closer. 'Allow me, Miss Brentwood. Stand quite still. I will have you free in no time at all.'

Camilla felt her breath catch in her throat as she looked down on Lord Westlake as his masculine fingers delicately unhooked each fibre of muslin from its capturing thorn. It was such a simple thing he was doing, but it seemed so intimate . . . and her heart was racing. Why did he have this effect on her? Why, if it were her brother Ralph unhooking her dress from the thorns, she would be pulling away impatiently. Yet, with Lord Westlake, the same action was making her breathless with . . . what? Anticipation?

She felt a prickle of desire flow over her skin. Her fingers ached to reach out and caress his hair where it curled onto the collar of his coat, and she had to clasp them together to stop them from doing so. Her unmaidenly thoughts brought a rosy hue to her cheeks and she was glad that Lord Westlake's attention was upon the hem of her gown.

Too soon, the task was done and Lord Westlake smiled up at her. There was a strange look in his eyes — almost bewilderment. Was he affected in the same way as she was? Her mouth felt quite dry and involuntarily she moistened her lips with the tip of her tongue.

Lord Westlake laughed a little shakily and he spread out his arms.

'I compliment you, Miss Brentwood. Here we are, only recently agreed to be friends, and I am already at your feet!'

Camilla wondered if there was more than banter in his voice and she was unsure how to proceed. Her sense of amusement came to her aid and she laughed merrily. 'Then, do get up, Lord Westlake, or you will have Mama thinking you are making another declaration!'

Jack put his hand against his heart in dramatic fashion. 'Ah! Alas, you have already turned me down once. I am not sure if I could bear to be refused a second time.' He rose to his feet, a merry gleam in his eyes. 'May I, instead, invite you to come driving with me later this afternoon when I have concluded my business with banker Hurley?'

'That would be — oh!' Her face fell. 'I am sorry, I am meeting a number of my friends at the Assembly Rooms in town to finalise our plans for the Vicarage Garden Party that is to be held a week on Saturday. I trust you will be attending, m'lord?' She was thankful to have found such a mundane topic to talk about and her tongue ran on artlessly. 'Your grandfather used to open the fete, and everybody goes — all the villagers and families from miles around. In fact, we were only saying the other day that we need to look over the folding tables and chairs and other items we generally use.

'They are stored in one of your outbuildings. With you being away, we have not had the opportunity to discuss the arrangements with you, although I am sure that your outdoor men will have it all in hand already.'

Jack also felt some relief. He was taken aback by the intensity of his emotion and was unprepared for how best to proceed in that direction.

'Then we must arrange a suitable time for that to be done. Maybe Sunday afternoon would suit? It is a time when everyone will be free. Why not ask all concerned if they would like to come to Kelsham Hall at about two o'clock to see what's what? And afterwards we shall have a picnic. I am sure Mrs Winslade will be able to provide a fine spread.'

He awaited her answer with such an intensity in his eyes that it made her limbs feel weak. Camilla blushed prettily. She knew her feelings towards him were undergoing a change. Was she falling in love? Of that she was not entirely sure. Yet she had never known her heart to leap and flutter in the way it was now doing.

'I shall do that, my lord, and let you know what they say.'

'Splendid.' He looked at her quizzically, his gaze making Camilla's heart race again. A tiny gasp escaped her lips when he reached out and took hold of her hand. 'There is another small thing I would ask of you, Miss Brentwood. I grow rather weary of everyone calling me 'Lord Westlake' and 'm'lord'. As a friend, do you think you might get used to calling me by my given name? I have already asked your brother to do so. It is Jack, as you may remember.'

Indeed she did remember. It suited him, somehow. However, she was not sure what her mama would think of her using his given name so freely. Nor was the giddiness she was experiencing at the closeness of their bodies — and the way the conversation was going — consistent with being thought of in the same way as her brother. What was she feeling, for heaven's sake? For once, she was at a loss. Was this what it felt like to be falling in love? She needed to confer with Susannah.

'I am ... not sure it would be ... appropriate, m'lord,' she stammered, glancing down, embarrassed at the indecision she felt. It was so unlike her!

Lord Westlake smiled, squeezing her hand gently. He reached out with his other hand and placed a finger under her chin, tilting her face towards him. 'Then, at least do me the honour of simply calling me Westlake,' he suggested softly.

Camilla swallowed. His lips were so close and she felt her gaze drawn irresistibly to them. She was sure that if she were to raise herself on to her tiptoes, he would lower his head and their lips would meet. The thought of the sweet bliss that would ensue was almost overwhelming. Her lips tingled and she moistened them with the tip of her tongue.

Tempted though she was, she knew it would be a disgraceful thing to do and she pushed the thought away, giving her head a little shake as she steadied herself.

'That . . . that would be . . . more acceptable,' she breathed.

'Good.' He picked up the basket of roses and extended his other arm towards her. Camilla placed her hand upon it and, after exchanging a brief but intimate smile, they made their way towards the house.

# 8

As he drove away, Jack's heart felt strangely light and the future seemed promising. All he had to do was to bring this business with Hurley to a satisfactory conclusion, and he would be able to concentrate on his own personal future.

His visit to London had been very promising. Firstly, Coutts could find no record of the company Hurley proposed he invest in, indicating it was a fraudulent proposition. Secondly, he had hired investigators to discover any moneylenders with whom Hurley might have been dealing, in Bristol and Bath as well as in the capital, and had already started to purchase any papers so discovered. And, thirdly, a former Bow Street Runner with a good reputation for honest dealings was already at work on his behalf discovering how many local businesses in Kelsham were in Josiah Hurley's hands.

Furthermore, he planned to settle his own temporary loan that very afternoon — hopefully without alerting Hurley to the fact that his affairs were under such scrutiny.

After a light luncheon, he ordered his town carriage to be made ready and he arrived at the bank promptly at two o'clock. He was ushered into the inner sanctum without delay. A portfolio lay opened on the desk.

'Ah, good day, m'lord,' banker Hurley greeted him amicably. 'I trust your visit to the capital met with your expectations.'

'Things couldn't have gone better,' Jack responded airily, waving his hand in the air as he seated himself unbidden. 'Seems I wasn't in dibs as much as I feared — and a couple of fortuitous evenings at White's have more than replenished my pocket!' He withdrew a slim packet from his inner pocket. 'You will be relieved to know that this draft on my account at Coutts will pay off the loan from you and put my account back into good standing.'

'Oh . . . er . . . well done,' Hurley managed to congratulate him, though without conviction. 'And enough to cover the investment we discussed?' he added hopefully, pushing the prepared document across the desk. 'It only requires your signature . . . here . . . and here. I shall get my clerk to come in to witness it.'

Hurley rose from his seat, but sank back again when Jack responded, 'I'm afraid I have changed my mind about that, Hurley. Coutts advised against investing in new companies at the moment, especially with all I intend to do to bring Kelsham Hall into the nineteenth century. Got to learn to act the responsible landowner, hey!' He laughed affectedly, as if such a notion was beyond expectation. 'And I cannot go against my bankers' advice, can I? Got to bow to their better judgment!'

'Huh! Banks like Coutts will never

make their way in the world with an attitude like that!' Hurley protested. 'Don't let them tie your hands, man. Tell 'em it's your money and you can do as you please with it. Why, your fortune would have been double its size, had the old lord heeded my advice!' His eyes suddenly took on a look of calculation. 'I tell you what I am prepared to do. Instead of paying off your temporary loan, why don't you invest that money instead? You'll have doubled it in no time at all and can settle your loans then. What d'you say, m'lord?'

Jack spread his hands in a helpless gesture: 'Unfortunately it is all tied up until I am thirty years of age. Still, that is less than a year away. Who knows what I might do then?' He let the carrot of a possible future deal dangle before the banker. 'Until then, it appears that I have to do my dealings through them. With not knowing his heir, my grandfather apparently did not want to take any chances.'

Jack managed to seem boyishly rueful about this revelation, though, in fact, he was heartily glad that the safety measures had been put into place, since it enabled him not to alienate Hurley, nor scare him into doing something desperate. 'So, shall we sign the necessary papers to clear my loans?' he suggested mildly.

Once this was done, he pushed back his chair and rose to his feet. Before he could utter his words of farewell, however, the door burst open and Mrs Hurley and her daughter bustled into the office, followed by a protesting clerk.

'Ah, Lord Westlake! You are returned at last!' Mrs Hurley declared in some reproof. She waved a dismissive hand at the clerk. 'Do tell this impertinent man to get back to his work, Mr Hurley. He had the effrontery to try to forbid me access to my own husband!'

Hurley waved the cringing clerk away, whilst his wife concentrated on chiding Lord Westlake over his visit to London.

'I hope your visit to the capital lived up to your expectations, m'lord, after abandoning us so precipitously!' Her manner was rather haughty, still smarting as she was from what she believed to be his trickery in persuading them to believe he was more flush in the pockets than was the case.

'Lord Westlake has had a successful trip to London, my dear,' Hurley hastened to intervene, aware that the peer's return to fortune made him once more an 'eligible parti' for his daughter to chase and wed. 'He is just about to take his leave,' he added meaningfully.

Mrs Hurley's eyes brightened at once. She wagged a playful finger at his lordship. 'Ah, you naughty boy! You were teasing us with your tales of being at low ebb! Well, never mind, we shall forgive you, shan't we, Dorothea? Now, how fortunate that you have concluded your business here, m'lord. Dorothea was feeling a little faint, weren't you, dear? We intended to persuade Mr Hurley to finish early here in order to drive us home, but I am sure that you will do just as well. How fortunate that you have your town carriage outside.'

Jack was too well-mannered to refuse and bowed politely. 'Of course, ma'am, Miss Hurley. It will be my pleasure.'

His business with the banker concluded for the time being, he allowed the ladies to precede him into the reception area and then gallantly offered them each an arm.

'So kind of you to take us home, Lord Westlake,' Mrs Hurley declared loudly, at the same time acknowledging the bows from other clients, as did Lord Westlake. 'You will take tea with us, of course.'

With much fussing, the ladies were finally settled onto the seat of his carriage and Jack was thankful to climb up onto the driving seat and be on his way at last.

That his reappearance in town had been noted was evident by the number of open stares and bows that his progress along the main street generated. From the gloating comments he could hear from his two passengers, he knew that they were relishing their part in the spectacle. Jack bore them no ill-will. Let them enjoy it, if that was their means of pleasure. They were, he did not doubt, innocent victims of Mr Hurley's malpractices.

As they were leaving town, he noticed a curricle speeding erratically towards them. As it drew closer, he recognised George Hurley at the reins and his eyes immediately shifted to Hurley's passenger. He smiled broadly and immediately drew his chestnuts to a standstill, raising his hat.

Miss Brentwood touched Hurley's arm, no doubt drawing his attention to the presence of his mother and sister in Jack's carriage. Hurley pulled heavily on the reins, bringing his greys to a skittering halt.

Jack beamed disarmingly. 'Hurley. Miss Brentwood,' he greeted them. 'A mighty fine day for a drive, is it not?'

'Westlake,' George curtly returned the greeting. He nodded towards his mother and sister. 'Mama. Dorothea.'

129

Mrs Hurley returned the greetings and bowed her head civilly towards Camilla. 'Good day, Miss Brentwood!' She prodded Jack with her parasol. 'George couldn't wait to take Miss Brentwood in his new curricle, Lord Westlake! What a delightful couple they make, do they not? They have been such friends since childhood. Isn't that so, Miss Brentwood?'

Camilla's eyebrows rose slightly. 'Indeed, ma'am,' she responded politely, still holding on to the edge of her seat as the pair of greys skittered impatiently. She hoped his lordship did not take Mrs Hurley's comments to mean more than they ought. She smiled boldly at him. 'Lord Westlake, everyone thanks you kindly for your invitation to come to Kelsham Hall on Sunday afternoon to sort out the items for the vicar's Garden Party — and to the picnic, later.'

'I am looking forward to it,' Jack agreed. 'Mrs Winslade has promised us a fine spread.'

'A picnic? Oh, how delightful!' Mrs

Hurley cried. 'What an excellent notion! D'you hear that, Dorothea? A picnic at Kelsham Hall! We are on the Garden Party committee, Westlake, and will be pleased to come along. I expect the invitations are awaiting us at home?'

'It was quite an impromptu arrangement, Mrs Hurley. A working party, you understand. Anyone who wishes to come may do so. It will be quite informal; no ceremony. Just arrive when you wish and someone will direct you to wherever we are.'

'Oh.' Disappointment at such an offhand invitation temporarily flattened her voice, but she swiftly rallied. 'Then we must hurry home so that we can choose what to wear, Dorothea. Oh, how exciting!'

George grinned at Jack. 'Enough about picnics! Leave that to the women, eh, Westlake. What d'you think of my new rig? Got it just the other day, you know.' He grinned slyly and added in a conspiratorial fashion, 'Put my winnings to good use, what? And new cattle as well! Prime bits of blood, ain't they? I wager they'd easily outrun your pair! Shall we test it out? Just your rig against mine?'

Jack eyed the restless greys, reflecting wryly that Hurley's purchase had been at his expense. Still, it had served its purpose. 'I'd wait until you have got them settled, Hurley, if I were you,' he advised. 'And go easy on their mouths. From the look of them, I'd say they are harnessed too tightly.'

'Nonsense! High-spirited, that's all. I like 'em with spirit . . . just like women, eh?' He guffawed. 'Look at 'em now! Impatient to be off! Must go, Mother.' George's face was perspiring with the effort of keeping his greys under control. 'Eager brutes, aren't they? G'day, Westlake!' And, with a shake of the reins, he gave his pair their head.

Jack raised his hat to bid farewell, swinging around in his seat to watch their departure. He saw Miss Brentwood clutch at her bonnet with her right hand, whilst holding tightly to her seat with the other. A flash of concern for her safety diminished the warm smile that had lit his face for the duration of the short conversation.

He was brought back to the present when Mrs Hurley said sharply, 'Lord Westlake! My daughter would like to proceed.'

'Pardon? Oh, yes, ma'am. My apologies, Miss Hurley.'

He gently flicked the reins and they smoothly set off once more.

He was not to know that the short meeting had confirmed alarm bells that were already ringing in Mrs Hurley's mind; nor that she later admonished her son and daughter on the subject dearest to her heart.

'Dorothea, you must make much more of your chances to seize Westlake's attention. Miss Brentwood monopolises him far too much!'

'But what can I do, Mama? He barely looks at me when Miss Brentwood is around.' Dorothea pouted.

'Then you must thrust yourself

before him! *Make* him notice you. Trip over at his feet; swoon into his arms; lure him into a private room. Miss Brentwood managed to find herself alone with Westlake, dressed in his housekeeper's clothes, and foolishly wasted the opportunity. So use your imagination, girl! And you, George, must make more of an effort to secure Miss Brentwood's affections for yourself — for, unless you do so, I fear she will snatch Westlake away from your sister. You must make sure of her without delay!'

George did his best to obey his mama, but Camilla's objective was to pursue a variety of social activities with as many of her friends as possible, giving her deepening friendship with Lord Westlake ample room to develop naturally. Since Ralph had now been declared fit enough to rejoin his regiment and was to travel to London three days before the Garden Party, he was happy to accompany her to the various social engagements with their

mutual friends; giving Camilla the freedom to refuse with an easy conscience
George's many offers to be her driver.

It suited Jack to follow a similar
scheme, and he was careful to spread
his attentions between all the young
ladies present at the various functions
they attended. He purposely arrived
slightly late to a musical soirée at the
Assembly Rooms in Helsham so that he
could remain standing near the back,
and was certain that none of the
watching chaperones knew which particular lady later gave him the greatest
delight by her sparkling repartee; and
he danced with practically every eligible
young lady at a charity ball in Bath,
causing all the mamas and chaperones
to look upon him with a favourable eye.

Camilla's dance card was more than
three-quarters filled by the time Westlake arrived at the ball. Two dances
had been taken almost immediately
by George, though she did refuse his
requests for more, including the supper
dance.

'No one will take it amiss of us, Cammy,' he had tried to persuade her. 'In fact, I am sure it is almost expected of us.'

'And I am sure it is not,' Camilla replied firmly. She was determined to have some spaces free for Westlake — providing he asked, of course!

She was aware the moment he made his entrance, and experienced the now familiar fluttering of her heart when they were in the same company. She managed to appear unconcerned when his entry was checked by Mrs Hurley, who had positioned herself and Dorothea at the entrance to the ballroom. Mrs Hurley hailed his lordship before he had even had opportunity to glance around. Camilla watched the exchange wryly, knowing with complete certainty that the significant supper dance was now spoken for.

She engaged Charlotte in bright conversation, but was fully aware of Westlake's progress as he made his way around the room, greeting his many new friends and acquaintances and delighting the mamas by requesting their daughters' cards.

Eventually, he reached her and made his bow. She was sure there was a special twinkle in his eyes. She bobbed a small curtsey and was happy to give him her card so that they might compare spaces. He selected the cotillion and a country dance.

Later, when she and Westlake promenaded down the set together, conversation flowed naturally between them, with none of the false gallantry many of the young men learned by rote. She knew she was falling in love at last. And she was sure he felt the same, though he had made no mention of wishing to speak with her father. Was she reading more than he intended in his manner towards her? Was a similar hope burgeoning in any other young lady's heart? She hoped not . . . or, if it were, she hoped it was unfounded.

★   ★   ★

On Sunday afternoon, George Hurley conveyed his mother and sister to Kelsham Hall, knowing that his sister had every intention of furthering her pursuit of Westlake during the course of the afternoon. Convinced that Camilla's displays of impatience with him were merely maidenly ruses intended to increase his ardour, George was determined to finally persuade her to receive his proposal of marriage.

They arrived to find a group of young men busily employed sorting out a stack of miscellaneous trestles and planks of wood that would be assembled into makeshift tables, and an assortment of benches and chairs for seating. Lists had been compiled at previous committee meetings and areas of responsibility shared out among the volunteers. The bran tub, the halfpenny race board, the maypole and rolls of canvas used to construct various side-shows were unearthed from their storage places.

Two large wagons had been pulled

into the yard and were ready to be loaded when the decisions over which items were needed had been made. Jack's outdoor men had made a start on dragging everything out of storage into accessible places and were standing by, ready to lift anything that any of the eager young men might want in a better place.

The ladies were sorting out the bunting flags and had gathered together an assortment of cloths that would cover the trestles and tables. There were exclamations of delight over the discovery of such as the hoopla rings and the stands to hold a selection of coconuts that were procured each year from the warehouses of Bristol; and when a sack of very old riding boots was opened, there was much laughter as they all recalled the rivalry displayed by the young men when it came to seeing which of them could throw one the furthest.

George delivered his mama and sister into this arena of activity, but they hovered on its periphery, their fine gowns obviously not suited to such work.

Seeing them, Camilla tried to draw them in. 'Would you like to take over ticking these items off this list, Miss Hurley?' she invited.

Dorothea looked disdainfully at Camilla, whose hands were now covered in dust, one of her cheeks bearing the mark of a dusty smear. 'Oh . . . no, thank you,' she declined, twirling her parasol with hands and arms encased in long white muslin gloves. 'I think Mama and I will seek out Lord Westlake. He said someone would direct us to where he happened to be when we arrived. We are his personally invited guests, you know.'

'Really?' Leticia Houghton raised an eyebrow and grinned impishly, nodding towards the open-ended upper level of that particular building. 'He is in the loft, up there. Shall I ask someone to assist you up the ladder?'

'Indeed not!' Dorothea retorted indignantly.

Someone laughed and Dorothea's

cheeks flushed angrily.

'Come, Dorothea! This is no place for us,' Mrs Hurley said sharply, tapping her arm. 'We shall find the other ladies and stroll around the garden until it is time for the picnic.'

Dorothea swung around and found herself face to face again with Camilla. 'You won't win him, you know!' she hissed in Camilla's ear as she passed by. 'Papa has promised me!'

Camilla gaped at her, her face blank with surprise.

Coolly Dorothea looked her up and down, adding a little spitefully, 'Besides, have you seen the state you are in? When Lord Westlake chooses his wife, he will choose someone who knows how to be a lady!' She tossed up her chin and, twirling her parasol, followed her mother out of the barn.

George made a movement to follow them, but was forestalled by his mother. 'You stay here, George! I am sure you can help these . . . *young persons* in their task.'

It was another hour before the sorting was completed and Lord Westlake's staff took over the task of loading the wagons. By this time, Camilla, still smarting from Dorothea's spite, felt thoroughly aggravated by George's persistent attendance on her and she stalked inside, to the rooms laid aside for the young ladies to refresh themselves, bemoaning his excessive zeal.

'He's besotted with you, Camilla,' Leticia sympathised.

'Not with any encouragement from me!' Camilla complained. 'What am I to do? Wherever I turn, he is there.'

'You speak too kindly to him,' Susannah pointed out. 'Be more blunt.'

'I don't like to hurt his feelings. We have known each other for ever . . . but he never used to be like this.'

'I think he accepted that you were always more friendly with Tim than with him. Maybe he thought you would turn to him when Tim went away?'

They emerged together onto the terrace overlooking the side lawn and an ornamental lily pond edged with stone, to join some of their parents who had come along as chaperones. Two long trestle tables were laden with platters of small sandwiches, cooked meats, slices of game pie, salads, cakes, scones, dishes of fruit and jugs of Mrs Winslade's freshly-made lemonade.

George was hovering close by, with two filled plates in his hands. Camilla couldn't help addressing him in exasperation.

'Thank you, George. Now, if you don't mind, I am going to join my friends over there. My *female* friends,' she added with emphasis. She took the plate from his hand and walked determinedly away.

An hour or so later, people were beginning to make their farewells as they sorted themselves into convenient carriage parties. Lionel and Ralph went to fetch the Houghton and Brentwood carriages. Camilla and her mother sauntered down towards the lily pond to remind the two Yardley girls that it was time to leave. Westlake strolled towards them.

'Thank you for informing me about my part in all this,' he smiled at Camilla, indicating the scene with his hand. 'I am quite glad to have my first function as lord of the manor over and done with, informal as it was.'

'And delightfully done,' Eleanor Brentwood complimented him. 'Your grandfather would have been proud of you.'

'Thank you, ma'am. The remains of the picnic will be parcelled up as soon as everyone has gone, and sent to the villagers. So, I will bid you ... What the dickens!'

The Brentwoods followed his gaze and saw Dorothea stepping daintily along the stone edging of the lily pond, which formed a natural focal point of that part of the garden, twirling her parasol in blithely carefree mood.

'What the devil is she doing?' Westlake said sharply. 'Can't she see the pavings are a little uneven?' He took a step towards her. 'Miss Hurley! Do take care!'

At his call, Dorothea swayed uncertainly for a moment, teetering on the very edge of the stone pavings . . . then, squealing, 'Oohh!' she stepped sideways into the pond.

The water in the lily pond was not deep; only about twelve inches at this time of year. Dorothea was now sitting in the pond with the folds of her skirt billowing around her as she flapped her arms up and down, squealing for help. Everyone froze for an instant. Then those who were nearby began to hurry forward.

Westlake was the first to reach the squealing young woman. As he stepped into the pond and reached down to take Dorothea's hand to pull her to her feet, Mrs Hurley hurried forward, crying, 'My poor girl! Save her, Lord Westlake! Save her!' Her face was glowing and Camilla could not help thinking that the whole episode had been choreographed. Even so, she could not help smiling. Dorothea's wet and muddy gown was adorned with clinging, slimy green weeds.

The next moment, Dorothea swayed towards Lord Westlake with a faint cry, leaving him little option but to sweep her up into his arms. Dorothea's hands clung around his neck as he clambered awkwardly out of the pond.

'There we are, Miss Hurley!' Westlake said cheerfully, stooping slightly in order to set her feet down onto the ground. 'Not much harm done! Though I expect you gave the frogs and snails a bit of a fright. And your gown is irretrievably damaged, I'm afraid.'

'Frogs and snails!' Dorothea cried, her hands still clasped about Lord Westlake's neck. Her face became a picture of horror. 'Mama! You didn't tell me there were . . . oooh!' Dramatically, she went suddenly limp in his lordship's arms.

'Never mind about frogs and snails, sir!' Mrs Hurley cried shrilly, her eyes glittering with annoyance. 'My daughter needs to be taken somewhere private where she might be bathed and changed out of her ruined clothes, before she perishes of cold!'

'Of course, ma'am. I'll take her indoors immediately. Where is your son, ma'am? He will need to bring your carriage to the front, so that he might take you and your daughter home as soon as she is recovered.'

Mrs Hurley smiled. 'I'm afraid George has already departed in our carriage. But I am sure your lordship will oblige us once again in our hour of need, won't you, sir?'

# 9

If Mrs Hurley had hoped that Dorothea might somehow contrive to be alone with his lordship and cause him to compromise her honour, she was to be disappointed. Swiftly Eleanor Brentwood took charge of the situation and helped Mrs Winslade to organise a private room where Mrs Hurley could oversee any ministrations offered to her daughter.

After much fussing and expressions of profuse gratitude to his lordship for his gallant rescue of 'dear Dorothea', Mrs Hurley was eventually persuaded to conduct her daughter into his carriage and be driven home to Larkspur Lodge. There, Lord Westlake managed to decline Mrs Hurley's pleas that he step inside so that Mr Hurley could add his thanks for his lordship's gallantry, by pleading the amount of clearing-up that had to be overseen back at Kelsham Hall.

'Well, I'm sure that is very noble of you, m'lord . . . though I would have thought your servants should be able to manage adequately without you.' Mrs Hurley pouted, adding with a sigh, 'Though it must be said that a house without a mistress is always at the mercy of lazy servants! I am sure you will be rectifying that lack in the near future, m'lord.'

'Indeed,' Jack responded. 'Good day, ladies. I am happy to have been of assistance to Miss Hurley and trust she will suffer no lasting distress.'

He took his leave and was soon on his way back to Kelsham Hall, reliving the happy atmosphere that had pre-vailed throughout the afternoon and feeling that his standing among his neighbours had taken a step forward.

He would not have felt quite so satisfied, had he been privy to a conversation between Mrs Hurley and her daughter later that evening.

Dorothea responded with irritation as her mother fussed over her and chivvied the servants into a scurry of activity, lighting a fire in the bedroom and preparing hot broth for her consumption. Although it had been very pleasant to be held in Lord Westlake's arms, the sole object of his attentive care for a few moments, she did not feel that her plan to attract his tender feelings towards her had advanced sufficiently for her to be complacent about it — even though he had indicated that he was, indeed, seeking a wife. Why did he not notice how much she longed for him to choose her?

Her indignation arose as she considered the way Mrs Brentwood had pushed herself forward to take charge. It had been vulgar in the extreme! Why, she had behaved as though her daughter were already assured the honour of becoming the next Lady Westlake. And that was not going to happen. It was to be *her* position! Lord Westlake was hers, and no one else's. It was not to be borne.

Her recent dreams had been full of tender love scenes between them, and when she was being held in his arms it had felt as though they were coming true. She remembered the fragrant, woody scent of him. It still assailed her senses. Her hands had clasped lovingly around his neck, her fingers gently entwining the curling ends of his hair. She had felt the warmth of his breath on her cheeks when he spoke to her . . . words that had been altogether too cheerful for her liking in the circumstances!

She leaned back against the plump feather pillows and wrapped her arms around herself, trying to recapture the sensations she had felt coursing around her when she was in his arms. With her eyes closed, she could imagine that his hands were touching her skin . . . her *bare* skin, she dared to imagine. It was such a lovely, delicious thought that a small cry escaped her as her own hands brushed across her breast.

'What is it, dear?' her mama asked

anxiously, hovering over her.

Dorothea opened her eyes, startled that the eyes looking down at her belonged to her mama and not to Lord Westlake. 'Oh! It was . . . ' She hesitated, breathing rapidly. She closed her eyes and took a deep breath, her hand lingering on her breast. Then her eyes flew open as she recognised the enormity of what she was about to say.

'I . . . I was just thinking of when Lord Westlake carried me from the lake, Mama — when he *touched* me.'

Her mother stared at her uncomprehendingly for a moment; then a light of realisation gleamed in her eyes. 'He *touched* you, Dorothea? Where? Where did he touch you?'

Dorothea laid her hand on her breast. 'Here, Mama. He touched me here.' She blushed. 'It did seem very . . . pleasurable . . . but I can't help thinking that a gentleman ought not to touch a lady there, unless he is promised to her.'

Her mama drew back and, for a

moment, Dorothea feared she had angered her and felt a stab of alarm. But then, a strange smile lit her mama's face. 'Did he, indeed? Well, you clever girl, we shall see what your papa has to say about that!'

★ ★ ★

Jack was surprised when Russell came into the dining room just after nine o'clock the following morning and announced that Mr Josiah Hurley had asked to speak with his lordship. 'Demanded' was probably the more accurate word, but Russell forbore to acquaint his master with that. No doubt his lordship would discover for himself that this was no social call. He sighed, wondering whether the rumours about his master's monetary affairs bore an element of truth.

'I have shown him into the library, m'lord.'

Jack wiped his lips with his napkin and rose from his seat. No doubt the banker wished to add his effusive thanks over his so-called 'gallant rescue' of his daughter the previous day. Best get it over with, and then he could proceed with his plans for today.

Hurley was standing with his back to the portrait of the late lord and, from his angry demeanour, Jack instantly knew this call was not what he had supposed. Had the banker discovered that he was investigating his business and was also in the process of buying his promissory notes of hand? He hoped not. It was too soon for him to be able to put in any safety measures to lessen the blow to many clients that the premature fall of the bank would undoubtedly cause.

The two men bowed curtly. Jack spoke first.

'Good morning, Hurley. You wish to speak with me.'

'Indeed I do, Westlake! You cannot be surprised, after your ungentlemanly behaviour yesterday. I am disappointed in you, lad . . . but I have no wish to quarrel with you. No doubt you were overcome with temptation and will be willing to rectify your honour!'

Jack shook his head. It could not be about the banking enquiries.

'My honour? I am sorry. I do not follow you. The only incident I recall happening yesterday was when I assisted Miss Hurley from my lily pond and carried her indoors. I assure you that we were never alone. Mrs Hurley was present the whole time, and other people no more than a step away.'

'You insulted my daughter, Westlake! Maybe ways are different in America but in this country, gentlemen do not mishandle young ladies of gentle birth — not unless they are prepared to put things right.'

Jack regarded him coldly. He was still in ignorance of his supposed offence, but he could guess which way this conversation was going. 'What am I accused of doing?' he demanded.

'You know damn well, m'lord! You touched her . . . *inappropriately*. In front of witnesses, you treated her no better than a light-skirt! I demand you take the necessary step to restore my daughter's honour, sir.'

Jack almost laughed at the ludicrous accusation, but managed to control the impulse. 'I lifted her out of my lily pond and carried her into my home — all at your wife's insistence, I may add. There was no other way to get her to a place of comfort and privacy, since she affected a swoon in my arms. But I adamantly deny any improper behaviour!'

'My wife and daughter say otherwise. My daughter's reputation is at stake. I demand satisfaction, sir!'

Jack took a deep breath. He knew the accusation was false. It was a ridiculous bluff. He forced himself to speak calmly. 'Very well, I will apologise to Miss Hurley for her perceived hurt. I can do no more.'

Hurley's face turned purple with rage. He jabbed an agitated finger at Jack. 'You will do a great deal more than apologise, m'lord! I demand an immediate proposal of marriage for my daughter!'

Jack was shaken. He knew that Hurley was seeking a way out of his financial difficulties and had his eye on Westlake money. He drew himself upright, his eyes cold with fury.

'I emphatically deny touching your daughter inappropriately, Hurley, and I refuse to be trapped into offering for Miss Hurley's hand in marriage by such scurrilous lies!'

Hurley's lips curled in derision. 'You refuse to rectify a lady's honour, your lordship? I shall drag your name through mud and mire!' His voice rose in blustering indignation. 'I shall make sure you are not received in any honourable company, sir! You will be the scorn of the county!'

Jack managed a harsh laugh. 'You will have to do a lot better than that, Hurley. You know the accusation is untrue, and I am certain that none of the witnesses of the incident would say otherwise. I suggest you find corroboration of your accusation before you attempt to besmirch my name. Now, if you have no more to add, I must ask you to leave. Good day, sir.'

Jack pulled the bell rope and Russell appeared in the doorway. Hurley had no option but to depart, albeit still mouthing threats of, 'I will see you ruined, sir! Ruined! D'you hear?'

Jack took a deep breath. He doubted Hurley would risk ruining his daughter's reputation by spreading such blatant lies, but the incident meant he must make a tactical retreat to London to hasten on the enquiries there — and bring Hurley to his knees before he absconded with whatever funds were still at his disposal.

He glanced at the ormolu clock on his mantelpiece. If he hurried, he would be able to travel with Ralph Brentwood, whose journey to London in order to receive his orders to rejoin his regiment was already planned for that day. He bounded upstairs, calling to his valet as he went.

Over the next few days, George redoubled his efforts to make himself indispensable to Camilla. Although she tried to respond as far as friendship allowed, she knew that her forced gaiety was seen for what it was.

'I'm missing Ralph,' she protested, which was in part true.

'Yes . . . and that Westlake fellow! You are wasting your time there, Cammy. Mama is sure that he has gone to London to arrange a marriage settlement for Dorothea.'

Camilla felt as though all her breath had been sucked out of her. Surely she had misheard him? Her stricken eyes searched his face for a sign that he was jesting. She saw none.

Instead, with uncharacteristic gentleness, as if aware of the shock she had felt, he softened his voice as he added, 'Mama says he spoke with Father before he left. You had best forget him, Cammy.' He forced a laugh. 'You could settle for me . . . I would take care of you. You know how fond of you I am.' He seized hold of her hands. 'Marry me, Cammy! I could get a special licence. We could be wed before he returns! That'd show him, eh!'

But Camilla was too shocked to even listen. She pulled her hands free. How could she have so misjudged the situation? She had been so certain that Westlake's feelings for her were undergoing the same transformation that hers had for him. He had almost said as much! Had it been a charade to hide where his true feelings lay? But why bother? He was free to marry whoever he wished, was he not?

'I am sorry, George.' She almost choked. 'I know we have been friends for years . . . but I do not love you in that way. I am sorry, truly. May I ask you to leave? I . . . I need to . . . ' She could say no more and fled the room.

★ ★ ★

The Garden Party, looked forward to for so long, now loomed as an ordeal for Camilla. She felt as though everyone else knew how deceived she had been, and must be secretly pitying her — though no one made mention of it to her. She flung herself into a frenzy of busyness, dodging from one activity to another, helping to organise the races for the children and encouraging some of the younger ones as they tried their hand at the hoopla stall, the bran tub and the halfpenny racetrack.

She laughed at the volunteers who sat in the stocks and allowed village children to throw wet sponges at them and cheered the young men who threw riding boots with all their might. Excited children danced around the maypole and, later in the day, older dancers showed that they had not lost their skills as they wove intricate patterns with the coloured ribbons.

Surrounded by happiness but not part of it, her attention was caught by the sound of a child crying. It was a small boy with a scraped knee.

'Come with me,' Camilla immediately invited him, taking the child's hand. She led him into the vicarage via the kitchen door and left him with a maid who was at work there. As she re-emerged into the yard, George Hurley was awaiting her. He took hold of her arm.

'Camilla! Quick!' he hissed. 'It's Westlake. He needs your help!'

'Westlake?' Camilla echoed. 'Is he back from London? Why would he need my help?'

'He didn't say. He just wants me to take you to him. I think something must have happened in London.' He was hurrying her through the kitchen yard and turned towards the small stable yard, where his young groom was standing by the two greys harnessed to his curricle.

Camilla halted. 'But where is he? How did he contact you?'

'Er . . . a lad came with a message. He ran off as soon as he had delivered it. Come on, quickly, we have wasted enough time already! Up you get.'

He handed her up into the curricle and ran round to the driver's side, where he hastily seated himself. His groom leaped aboard as George flicked the reins and they made a smart exit from the stable yard.

'Camilla! Where are you going?'

Camilla looked back to see Susannah by the corner of the vicarage, her arm raised. All Camilla could do was wave a hasty farewell as George recklessly swung the curricle out through the gateway and along the road towards the town.

★　★　★

Lord Westlake was indeed back. At that moment he was in the inner office at Hurley's bank, towering intimidatingly over its manager.

'How . . . how dare you burst into my office in this manner, Westlake?' Hurley spluttered up at him. 'I sincerely hope you have come prepared to make my daughter an offer of marriage! And who are these men? I insist that they leave my bank!'

Jack placed both hands on the surface of the desk and leaned forward until his face was no more than a few inches away from Hurley's. 'I have news for you, Hurley,' he said calmly. 'This bank is no longer your bank; it is mine! As for these gentlemen, allow me to introduce them. Their names are Mr Brown and Mr Cartwright, official investigators of His Majesty's Government. They know a great deal about you, Mr Hurley. They have been looking into your affairs for a number of weeks and have come up with some surprising results.'

Hurley cowered back in his chair. 'I . . . I don't know what you are talking about! Get out before I have the law on you!'

'You have not been listening, Mr Hurley. Mr Brown and Mr Cartwright *are* the Law! They are here to take you into custody.'

Hurley's face underwent a number of

colour changes. 'On . . . on what charge?' he blustered. 'There is nothing . . . '

'How about fraudulent activities, for a start?' Jack suggested calmly. 'Encouraging your clients to invest in non-existent companies? Offering loans to cover the outlay, and then foreclosing on the loans when they had no means of repaying them? Shall I go on?'

'You . . . You're bluffing! This is just a cowardly way to distract attention from your insulting behaviour to my daughter. It won't wash, Westlake. Besides, this whole town will be bankrupted if you were to pull me down! Your name will be synonymous with ruin! Are you prepared to throw them all out on the street?'

'No, but it seems that you were. That is why I have bought the bank.'

'You cannot have! It's not for sale! Get out! Get out!'

Jack turned to one of the men standing behind him. 'Show him!'

Mr Brown opened the leather case that was in his hands and produced a handful of papers. 'Your notes of hand,

Mr Hurley. The papers relevant to the loans you have taken out — all legally purchased on behalf of Lord Westlake. According to our investigations into the affairs of this bank, these papers represent over eighty per cent of the collateral. The missing twenty per cent is irrelevant at the moment. It will, no doubt, be discovered when we scrutinise the books here.'

Hurley had paled. He recognised his own signature on the papers shown to him. Yet still he refused to accept his defeat. 'You cannot! I will not allow you access to my books. My clerks will burn them! No doubt they are already doing so.'

Jack straightened up. 'The books are already in the possession of more revenue officers. It's Fleet Street for you, I'm afraid.'

Hurley at last faced his downfall. He slumped back in his chair. 'I'm ruined!' His face reflected defeat. 'My wife! My son! My daughter! You cannot do it, Westlake. Your grandfather would not have seen them so disgraced! I've put no one out of their home, Westlake. Have you no pity?'

Jack thumped his fist down on the desk. 'You were about to cut and run, Hurley! The whole house of cards was about to come falling down. By your own admission, almost the entire township would have been ruined!'

He paused and straightened his body again, allowing his anger to drain from him. 'But you are right, I do have pity,' he admitted, his voice calmer. 'Your wife and family may remain in your house until everything is settled. If your house needs to be sold to offset any debts — and I see by your reaction that it will — a modest sum will be allowed for them to be housed. More than that, I cannot promise. Your victims' plights will take priority.'

Even that largesse did not satisfy Hurley. He decided to hit out in the only way left to him. 'As if you care! You're no more than a jumped-up pauper. You come to this town and expect everyone to fall at your feet

— even the lovely Miss Brentwood. Well, you're too late to get her! My son has at last decided to act like a man instead of grovelling at her feet like a mouse. She'll have to marry him, or be ruined! She'll . . . aargh!'

His gloating was cut off as Jack seized hold of his coat lapels and hauled him roughly to his feet. 'What has he done to her? If he has dared to touch her, I shall . . . '

'You will what? She will be out of your reach!'

'What has he done? Where has he taken her?'

Hurley sneered at him. 'So, now you, too, know how it feels to have lost?' He stood up. 'I have nothing more to say.' He looked at the other two men. 'I am ready to accompany you, gentlemen.'

Jack banged his hand down on the desk, making Hurley leap back in alarm. Jack glared at him contemptuously.

'Take him away!' he snarled at his two companions. 'I will be in touch.'

His face inscrutable, he strode

through the bank. What had Hurley done? What day was it? Saturday? It was the day of the vicar's Garden Party. Surely Miss Brentwood would be there, safe, surrounded by other people?

His town carriage was down the street at the side of the bank, where he had instructed his groom to lead the horses up and down. Jack strode to the corner and whistled inelegantly through two fingers. When the groom turned round, he raised his hand.

'Turn the carriage, lad! And hurry!'

As Jack ran down the street, he heard the sound of galloping hooves behind him. He glanced over his shoulder and saw a curricle speeding past the end of the street. His heart leaped. It was them! It was Hurley with Miss Brentwood at his side, clearly remonstrating with him. He was not too late, after all! He ran to meet his groom, seizing the reins from his hand as he leaped up onto the driving seat.

'Jump aboard, lad! And hold tight!' And he set off in pursuit.

George's driving skill had improved slightly since he had purchased his new curricle, but they were going at a cracking pace and the curricle swung from side to side. They had left the vicarage far behind and had travelled a quarter of a mile before Camilla could relax her hold on her seat and bring herself to again ask their destination.

'Er . . . somewhere on the outskirts of town,' George had said briefly, concentrating on the road.

Not wanting to distract his attention, Camilla waited a few minutes before asking again, 'Where exactly?'

'Leave it to me! I know where we're going!'

Camilla pondered a few more minutes, wondering why Westlake had involved George in his clandestine plan. 'Why did the messenger contact you?' she queried.

'I suppose I was the first person the lad saw,' George said reasonably. 'I didn't ask to be the one. In fact, I don't really want to take you to Westlake . . . but I thought it would be what you would want.'

'Hmm. Well, thank you, George.' She smiled at him, feeling guilty that she had misjudged him. Impulsively, she patted his arm. 'That was very thoughtful of you. I appreciate it . . . but I must admit I am very worried about what might have happened to make Lord Westlake send for me. In what way could I help him if he is in trouble? Did the boy give no clue about what has happened?'

'No. As I said, he ran off as soon as he passed on the message.'

Camilla chewed at her lower lip as she considered the implications. It was only as they sped through Helsham, at a speed far greater than was safe, that her suspicions and alarm became more focused.

'I thought you said Westlake is somewhere on the outskirts of town?'

'Er — I meant the far side . . . a bit nearer to Bristol,' George admitted.

'Bristol?' Camilla cried in consternation. 'You're telling me that Westlake is at Bristol? I can't go all the way to Bristol dressed only like this. We'll be gone for hours!'

'That's all right. One of Dorothea's cloaks is under the seat. Put it on if you are feeling chilled.'

Camilla narrowed her eyes. 'Why do you have Dorothea's cloak under the seat? She would not have expected to need it this afternoon.' Her suspicions deepened as George's cheeks stained red.

'You're pitching the gammon, aren't you? Your tale is a bag of moonshine!' She began to pummel his arm with her fists. 'Where are you taking me? You've abducted me under false pretences. Turn round immediately and take me home!'

George cowered away from her blows, lifting his left elbow to hinder her attack. 'Leave off, Cammy! I can't drive whilst you are attacking me. You will have us over if you carry on so!'

'Then pull over and turn around! If you think you can force me to marry you, you can think again. I would rather remain forever unwed than to marry you — especially after this trick you have pulled. I mean it, George! Your father will be livid!'

George faltered for a moment and Camilla thought she had persuaded him of his folly. But before she could press on with the advantage, he flicked his whip more furiously, urging his greys to a faster speed. Camilla was flung backwards by the increase in speed.

'Stop it, George!' she screamed. 'Pull over!' She managed to right herself and grabbed at his arm again. 'Stop at once, George! You'll have us killed if you carry on like this!'

'Father will have me killed if I do not!' he growled through his teeth, flicking his whip again. 'Let go of me!'

Camilla stared at him as his words sank in. 'Your father? What in Heaven's name do you mean?'

George took his eyes off the road. 'You must marry me, Cammy!' he implored. 'We are facing ruin. I have obtained a special licence. We are to be married on Monday. The scandal will soon be forgotten. I shall look after you, really I shall.'

They sped around a bend in the road and a flash of something shot into the road just ahead of them. It was a small dog that had emerged from an opening in the hedge, followed immediately by a young lad.

'George! Look out!' Camilla screamed.

The dog had no chance to avoid being hit. The horses skittered as their hooves trampled the small animal and George struggled to keep the pair under control. There was a sickening lurch as the wheels of the curricle ran over the already stunned animal.

At the same moment, a whir of movement at Camilla's left side made her swing around in her seat to look back over her shoulder. The lad lay in a crumpled heap at the roadside, only a few feet away from the mangled remains of his dog.

'Stop, George! You hit the lad!' she cried.

'Nonsense! We missed him by a mile.'

'No! You hit him!' She looked back

174

again. 'Look. He's trying to get up!' She clutched at his arm. 'You must stop! Or I . . . I will jump. I will!'

She rose from her seat. George pushed her down again.

'All right! All right!' He drew the horses to a stop but clamped his left hand over Camilla's right arm, restraining her from leaping down into the road. 'Look, Camilla, the lad fell, that is all. Boys scrape their knees every day! It's part of growing up, for goodness' sake. I am sorry about the dog, but the lad can get another one. Leave it. No one will know it was us.'

Camilla gaped at him. She could not believe she had heard him aright. She yanked her arm free of his grasp. 'Do as you please, George!' she said coldly. 'You will have to live with your conscience. I am going back to see what I can do to help.'

'You cannot!' He raised his arms to shake the reins but Camilla did not wait. She gathered her skirt in her hand and jumped.

# 10

Camilla stumbled as her feet hit the ground and she rolled over and over. Her shoulder hit the ground hard and she felt winded by the fall, but she managed to scramble to her feet and run back along the road towards the boy. He was still struggling to sit up and Camilla knelt at his side.

'Is he all right, Miss?' asked a voice above her. It was George's young groom. He dropped down beside her.

Camilla smiled at him gratefully. She had thought for a moment that the running steps indicated that George had come to his senses, but she was not entirely surprised that he had not. She glanced along the road, but George's curricle had gone.

The injured boy was trying to crawl to where his dog lay in a pathetic heap of fur and blood.

'Blackie!' he moaned. 'Don't be dead! Don't be dead!'

Hastily Camilla crouched at his side and gathered him into her arms, blocking his view of his dog. 'Hush, now! Hush! You cannot do anything for him. He would not have suffered. It was over so quickly.'

She hoped that her words were true. The lad seemed to take some comfort from them in any case. He turned towards her and buried his face against her chest. He was sobbing helplessly, his face pressed against her as she cradled him in her arms. She looked at his legs. One was obviously broken and its foot looked decidedly mangled.

She glanced at George's groom who was crouching helplessly beside her, his eyes wide with shock at the sight of the blood pumping from the lad's leg and mangled foot.

'What's your name, lad?'

'Dickie Smith, miss. I'm right sorry about this.'

'It's not your fault, Dickie. But I

need help. There is nothing we can do for the dog, I am afraid — but the lad's leg is in a bad way. I need you to run back to that farm we just passed.' She glanced down at the boy in her arms but he seemed too distraught to question. 'Try there. Tell them what has happened and ask for help.'

'Yes, miss.'

Dickie set off at a run and Camilla cradled the lad with one arm, rocking him with an instinctive soothing motion, murmuring, 'There, now! You will be all right. Just you see. We'll soon get you fixed up,' whilst, with her other hand she gripped hold of his leg just above the break, trying to stem the flow of blood.

'It 'urts, miss,' he sobbed. 'Ave I brok' it? I won't be able to 'elp me da' . . . an' 'e'll leather me for takin' Blackie out!'

'No, he will not. He will just be thankful that you are all right . . . and so you will be!'

Even as she whispered the words,

Camilla knew that his life would be much harder from now on. Even if his leg and foot were saved, he would be forever crippled, unfitted for life on a working farm.

The sound of a fast approaching carriage drew her attention and she looked up. It could not be George returning; it was coming from the opposite direction. She did not immediately recognise the horses but, as the vehicle drew nearer, she recognised the driver. Westlake! Her heart leaped. He was back! And he was safe.

When Jack rounded the bend in the road and saw the figure of a young woman seated in the roadway, he knew immediately that it was Miss Brentwood. He had driven his pair as hard as he could, but the country lane had many bends and twists and his town carriage was not as fleet as a curricle — not even one driven by the inept driver he knew George Hurley to be. From the occasional brief glimpse of them in the distance, he could tell that

Miss Brentwood was arguing with Hurley, probably telling him to slow down or even to stop.

Where was Hurley taking her? It was the direct road to Bristol, and Miss Brentwood had no maid with her. Was that what Josiah Hurley had meant when he had said 'She will have to marry him'? That his son was aiming to compromise her and thus force the marriage? Well, not if he had anything to do with it! He had urged his team on, desperately trying to gain ground on the erratically driven vehicle ahead.

Now, here was his darling sitting in the road ... and no sign of either Hurley or his curricle! What had happened? Had she decided to jump? Was she hurt? He drew to a halt some yards away and jumped down. He tossed the reins to his groom and hurried towards her.

'Miss Brentwood! Are you all right? What happened? Where is Hurley?' Streaks of blood marked her face and he thought for a moment that she was indeed injured. His gaze dropped to the dark bundle of clothes that she was cradling to her and he realised with shock that the 'bundle' was a roughly clad farmer's lad — and the bloodied mass of an animal lay a few feet beyond. It spoke of an accident of some sort — but not to Miss Brentwood. He felt vastly relieved. He longed to sweep her into his arms but knew his concern must rest on the injured boy for the time being.

A frown creased his brow. 'Did Hurley do this? Has he gone for help?' He crouched at her side. 'He should have left his groom with you.'

Miss Brentwood raised her face to him and he could see traces of tears.

'George was driving too fast as usual. He . . . he wasn't going to stop. I had to threaten to jump. His groom came with me. I have sent him back to the farm we had just passed to get help.' Her voice trembled. 'Will you take a look at this boy's leg and foot? I fear . . . ' She broke off, biting her lower lip with her teeth as more tears ran unheeded down her cheeks.

'Here!' He pulled out a handkerchief and handed it to her, at the same time replacing her hand with his own above the boy's ankle.

Camilla took the handkerchief from him but, instead of wiping her tears, she dabbed at the lad's face with it.

'See, Lord Westlake is here to help us,' she crooned softly. 'So, everything will be all right, just like I said.' She continued to rock the lad, holding him close, but looked over his head at Westlake. She shook her head, flashing a message of warning with her eyes. 'I think it needs . . . attention,' she said quietly.

Jack's main concern was for her, but he felt she was coping well — certainly she was not about to have hysterics, or faint. A surge of admiration shafted through him, but he tore his glance away from her and inspected the lad's leg. The broken bones protruded just above his ankle, and the foot was mangled out of recognition.

'Yes, I see what you mean.'

With one hand, he pulled off his immaculate cravat, shook it free of its folds and wrapped one end tightly around the boy's leg to ease the bleeding. The rest of it he folded around his ankle, giving the dangling foot some support.

'You did not explain where Hurley is. Has he gone to fetch a doctor?'

'No. He has just . . . gone,' she said in flat tones.

'Gone?' he echoed. The blank expression on her face deterred him from pursuing that question. 'Very well. Then let's get the lad into my carriage and get him to a doctor.'

Jack had just laid the lad carefully on one of the seats of his carriage and was handing Miss Brentwood up the steps, when three running figures appeared along the roads behind them — two men and a lad.

'Where's Jemmy? Where's my lad?' the older of the two men demanded, his face red with the exertion of running.

'He's here,' Jack told him. 'We are taking him to a doctor. Will you show us the way to the nearest one?'

'I can't afford no doctor!' the man protested. He scowled at Jack. 'Are you the cove who ran him down? This lad sez as how you was going far too fast! I hope as how you'll see to getting him right.'

'No, not him, mister!' Dickie protested.

'No, it was not I,' Jack affirmed. 'I have just come upon the accident but I am willing to help in whatever way I can. Are you his father? Good. Well, your son needs urgent help, so I suggest you climb into the carriage so that we can be on our way.'

\* \* \*

Eleanor was thankful that Camilla agreed to lie abed on Sunday morning. She suspected that some gossip would be in circulation and that speculation would be rife. Thankfully, Lord West-lake had kept his head and immediately sent word to them of his and Camilla's whereabouts. They were reunited with their daughter before most people were aware that anything was amiss and, hopefully, that was how the situation would remain. Westlake had promised to call to speak with Arthur before the day was over.

Not that Eleanor mentioned to her daughter any expectations she might have of that event when she entered her bedroom at mid-morning. Instead, she concentrated on the series of concerns at the Garden Party itself.

'What a to-do, there was!' she confessed in light tones, quite at odds with her feelings as the events had unfolded the previous day. 'First, Susannah came to tell us that you had driven away with George Hurley, after trying to avoid him all day. Then a messenger arrived with some news that obviously upset Violet. My heart almost stopped, for I feared it was to say you and George had had a carriage accident. But it was not — and she was driven away, hysterical, over something to do with the bank.'

'I wonder what that was about?' Camilla pondered, momentarily diverted from her own drama of the previous day. 'Does Papa know?'

'He has not said so, dear. Maybe we will eventually discover that from Lord Westlake, as he was seen striding from the bank immediately before he set off in great haste along the road to Bristol. He said that he would call here later today.'

Lord Westlake called at Greenacres just after two o'clock that afternoon and was shown into the library. Whatever was discussed in there had obviously reached an outcome that greatly pleased both gentlemen, as they were smiling and conversing with mutual bonhomie when they emerged and made their way to the drawing room. There Camilla, now dressed in a very pretty gown of pale blue sprigged muslin, was making some pretence at embroidering a sampler as she conversed somewhat nervously with her mother.

After making his bow and amicably greeting both ladies, Jack lowered his tall frame onto one of the conveniently placed chairs and elegantly crossed his ankles. He seemed to have a suppressed excitement within, as he calmly answered politely phrased questions about the events of the previous day and events leading up to it.

They were relieved to hear that the injured boy had had his broken leg reset and would remain in the care of an excellent Bristol doctor until he was fully recovered. They were astounded to hear what Lord Westlake had to say about the events at the bank concerning Hurley's fraudulent dealings — and Westlake's part in bring those dealings to light and to justice.

'So, you are now our bank manager as well as the lord of the manor!' Eleanor exclaimed. 'However will you find time to serve your customers well . . . in addition to putting your estate to rights?'

Westlake laughed. 'I shall not be doing the bank work myself, ma'am. I have employed an excellent manager to take charge for me there — one who will be answerable at all times to Coutts in London.' He smiled around. 'My intention is to spend as much time as possible on my estates, taking good care of my tenants, as a certain young lady pointed out to me, on my arrival, was my duty as the incumbent lord.'

Camilla blushed. So much seemed to have happened since then — and her feelings had much changed. But what were Lord Westlake's feelings concerning her? She felt they had been coming towards an understanding . . . but had recent events marred their budding friendship?

Lord Westlake caught her eye and her breath caught in her throat as she saw the intensity of his gaze. She knew her own feelings were clearly exposed upon her face and her heart fluttered as she sensed a similar response in Westlake's smile.

It was Eleanor who broke the silence between them. 'Let us take a stroll around the garden, Arthur,' she suggested, rising from the sofa. 'We will be within calling distance, and I am sure that all proprieties will be observed.'

'Indeed, ma'am,' Jack responded, rising politely to make a slight bow.

Jack remained standing as the older couple left the room. As soon as they had gone, he moved to stand in front of Camilla. She glanced up at him, her heart still racing and her throat unaccountably dry.

Suddenly shy, she cast her eyes down. It was clear that Westlake had asked for, and received, permission to address her — but did he really love her? Or was he simply seeking to protect her reputation?

Jack took hold of her hands and drew her to her feet, the pads of his thumbs gently caressing her knuckles. His eyes were tender with emotion and Camilla could feel her doubts melting away as his eyes told her more than words would ever express. Her breath caught in her throat.

'Miss Brentwood . . . Camilla . . . I have longed for this moment. I felt I could not ask for permission to address you until I had sorted out the malpractices at Hurley's bank, but you must know how I feel about you — how I have felt from almost the first moment I saw you.'

Camilla heard his words in breathless silence, her heart beginning to race as she took in what he was saying. 'Only 'almost'?' she teased, her eyes twinkling as she recovered her poise.

He grinned in response. 'At first, I believed you to be a youth . . . until I took hold of you.'

Camilla acknowledged his point with a rueful moue. 'And I thought you the most abominably arrogant young man I had ever had the misfortune to meet!' she said mischievously.

'I soon learned my error,' Westlake said softly, his thumbs still sending delightful sensations spiralling through her body. 'Have you had occasion to reconsider your first impression?'

'Mmm, a little,' Camilla murmured, glancing up at him through her eyelashes. 'Though I might need a little more persuading.'

'Might you indeed, my love? Have you any suggestions as to how we might set about that persuasion?'

He lowered his head towards her and Camilla's lips began to tingle in anticipation. She ran the tip of her tongue over them and raised her face with such trusting innocence that Jack's whole body leaped with desire. He drew her closer until it seemed as though their bodies were moulded together.

Camilla held her breath. Her legs seemed no longer to have the ability to hold her up and she was sure she would have sunk down to the floor, had not Westlake been supporting her. It felt so . . . intimate . . . so sensual . . . so excitingly wicked — yet so right. It was as if they were the only two people left in the whole world.

'I think,' she said breathlessly, 'that I am in the process of being persuaded right now!'

She could feel the warmth of his breath fan over her face, and a small moan of desire slipped unbidden from deep within her. Then all possibility of speaking was taken from her as his mouth claimed hers with such a soul-searing kiss that it left her trembling with emotion and weak with desire . . . and she knew that she was totally persuaded.

Not that she had any intention of saying as much. She was enjoying the persuasion so much that she wanted it to continue for the rest of her life!

## THE END

FAITH FOR THE FUTURE
A CHANGE OF HEART
ILLUSIONS OF LOVE
A DIVIDED INHERITANCE
ELUSIVE LOVE
THE FARRINGTON FORTUNE
A BRIDE FOR LORD MOUNTJOY
A LOVE WORTH WAITING FOR